Miss
Win

TALES *of* INTRIGUE *and* DECEPTION

ROSEMARY MAIRS

Paperback ISBN: 978-1-7384618-0-6
Ebook ISBN: 978-1-7384618-1-3

A catalogue record for this book is available from the British Library.

Cover and interior design by Damonza

For my mother and sister, with love

Contents

Angel

I ALWAYS GET AWAY with it.

Some would call it luck, or being in the right place at the right time, but it's more than that. People make it easy for me – they want to believe in what they see. The drunken tramp is given a wide berth, the skinhead shouting abuse, but not the young mother in the supermarket, the smart businessman.

Not a child.

It wasn't murder though, or even manslaughter. If it had been labelled, I suppose they would have called it negligence. I neglected to save her life. That is what a lawyer would have said in court. A jury would have been shocked by my youth – just ten years old! Such beautiful hair, they would have sighed, would have pictured my mother brushing it, her hands pausing on my shoulders, sharing a smile in the mirror.

Why, the court would have wanted to know. Why didn't you go for help? I could have told how she abused me, shown the bruises, but I didn't have any. If I had, I would have shown them long ago, to teachers, to whoever would look and listen.

Sometimes, I wanted her to beat me. She would vent all her anger and it would go away. I don't know why she hated me. Sometimes she would notice me and stare, as though I were a stranger walked in from the street. Her gaze would move to my hair, seeing how long it had grown, would look at it with disgust in her eyes.

I was so used to her silence, when she screamed for me the night she fell I didn't recognise her voice. I thought it was someone outside. She was lying on her back on the kitchen floor, an overturned chair beside the bench. She spoke quickly, as though making up for lost time, frantically telling me to get help. Her voice was clear, even with blood trickling from her head.

I went upstairs, got back into bed.

She made noise for a while.

In the morning I ran outside for help.

They put me in a home.

Plain sailing, once I got the measure of everyone. I did well at secondary school, was 'an exceptional pupil'; apparently university would carry me forward to a bright future.

A lecturer let slip personal info. I was his star student – asked the right questions, chatted after tutorials. Happened to mention how much I loved children. He told me about his two-year-old daughter. He and his wife went out a lot. Perhaps I'd like to babysit? He remembered what it was like living on a student grant.

He had done well for himself since. His wife had a chain of jewellery shops. She kept hers in a fancy glass box on her dressing-table. Should have known better; her shops were heavily alarmed. The insurance company thought the same, tried to get out of paying after the break-in. She proudly showed me her new safe, keyed the combination in front of me. Someone that stupid deserved to be robbed again, but I'd enough already to search for my father.

It would only be a matter of time, if I looked hard enough, but I'd always been fatherless, had nothing to go on. No birth certificate. They'd searched for it among my mother's belongings when I moved into the home, but couldn't find it.

I travelled from town to town. All I had was my mother's name. No one knew her. Why did I expect anyone to know her? As time passed I started to believe my own story – I had always been in the orphanage. She had died giving birth to me. My father had come to get me, but they'd turned him away.

I was in a café, my funds almost gone, when someone approached, asked if I minded sharing my table? He looked about fifty. There was something familiar about him – the shape of his face, similar colour of eyes to mine.

I could almost convince myself . . .

We went back to his house.

A father figure; better than nothing.

He brushed my hair each night in long, sweeping strokes. We shared a smile in the mirror, him unable to believe his luck at landing a twenty-year-old with golden hair to her waist and the face of an angel.

A registry office wedding.

He liked me at home, waiting for him, dinner on the table. Hanging out with my new friend Kyle didn't go down well. He wouldn't believe it was innocent, couldn't bear that Kyle was half his age.

'Months! We've only been married a few months!' He seemed to think his fists could pummel love for him back into me. I stopped seeing Kyle, but he'd got a taste for it, or maybe it was a reminder not to be a naughty girl again.

His company sent him away on business. Kyle poured me another glass of wine. We giggled like schoolchildren, would have the whole week together. He wouldn't be back until Friday.

We didn't notice him at first, at the bedroom door. Kyle started, tipped his glass – a pool of red on the sheet.

He grabbed me by the hair, pulled me off the bed, turned his attention to Kyle.

They were a good match.

It went on and on, until I got bored, picked up the bottle.

Kyle wouldn't stop sobbing afterwards. '*What have you done?*' he kept asking over and over. '*What have you done?*' 'It's all right. Go home,' I told him, as if a dead husband was an everyday problem for me, and he went, well, ran, actually. It took the police a while to find him. He was hiding in a derelict office block. They gave me protection – an officer outside the house – until they found him.

When the trial came to court the jury were slow coming to the obvious verdict. Kyle had been seen fleeing the house. He had motive, means and opportunity. Then of course there was my evidence. The trouble was, he didn't look the type – the boy next door. He cried as the judge passed sentence; some of the jury even looked upset.

He hadn't been as comfortably off, my husband, as I had thought. The house was rented, not his. The sale of the car, a few savings – enough for a cruise. The other passengers were mostly middle-aged couples. It was beginning to seem like a waste of time, but then he walked past my sun lounger. He stood at the railing, gazed at the ocean. His clothes were understated – chinos and a checked shirt – but he was rich. Extremely. Old money. I could smell it.

I wore a spectacular cocktail dress to dinner – black. I was a widow after all. But he didn't show. A heavily tipped waiter gave me some info. Randal Sinclair-Barret. His wife was dead; heart attack, something like that. He was taking his stroll one evening. The deck was deserted; everyone was inside, dancing, gambling. Someone was perched on the rail, poised to jump, the wind streaming her hair against the sky.

'You're very young,' his mother stated coldly, when we were introduced.

I exchanged a smile with Randal. 'Guilty as charged.'

She was still frosty when we announced our engagement.

The next day she wanted to see me, alone. Randal had never got over the loss of his wife, who he adored. I was merely a distraction. She was not going to let an upstart on the make ruin her son's life.

'Randal tells me you ride?'

Above the fireplace was a huge painting of a horse.

'I've always wanted to learn, but was too scared . . . seems a dangerous sport. I might take the plunge now. Perhaps we could ride together?'

'You won't get away with it.'

I had no idea what she meant.

'Making a fool out of my son. Out of me.'

Her eyes held mine, disgust radiating from them, until she could no longer bear to look at me.

I turned back to the painting.

'Randal wants me to have my portrait done. He says I have the face of an angel.'

A flutter of air, as she stormed from the room.

She was right of course.

Appearances are deceiving.

Hero

THE CLOCK IN Rob's hospital ward reached seven, and the first visitors arrived. Soon, Matt would be here; he would have to pull himself together to see his son. Rob watched the other patients welcoming loved ones, the smiles and holding of hands. It looked deceptively easy, this showing of affection, but it wouldn't be like that with Matt, especially not today, not on the day of Peter's funeral.

There was nowhere to hide. No way of avoiding this visit from his son. He could tell a nurse he didn't feel up to visitors, but that would be the coward's way out, and Rob had earned himself the reputation of a hero. Yesterday, Matt had sat silently beside his bed. Rob knew he was thinking what he had already said: 'You could have been killed as well.'

He would have been shocked if he had read his father's thoughts, if he'd known Rob was glad he couldn't go to the funeral, relieved that he didn't have to pay his respects. If only they had never met Peter, he kept thinking, if only he had never come to the farm looking for work.

'I'll take ye on a month's trial,' Rob had told him. What he really needed was someone with experience of dairying and sheep farming, not a student taking a year out to raise money to go to college.

When Matt left school to work on the farm full time they wouldn't need extra help. Lately, he'd been spending more hours indoors than out, doing his schoolwork, cooking their evening meals. They were getting by somehow, without Lorna. The house wasn't kept the way it used to be, or their clothes ironed, but they managed.

It was Lorna who had told Rob that Matt wanted to stay on at school to do A levels. He had been shocked. Matt was needed on the farm. What was the point doing more exams?

'He's thinking of doing accountancy,' Lorna had said.

They'd had this conversation in bed. Rob still wasn't used to sleeping alone. Even now, a year after her death, when he woke during the night he reached out his hand, expecting his wife to be lying beside him.

Her words came back to Rob as he saw the new lad's eagerness to learn about farming, how he gazed across the fields, a look of awe on his face at the view. Matt couldn't want to work in a town, to be stuck in an office all day. Farming was in your blood, everyone knew that.

Peter ate his packed lunch with them in the kitchen. Matt made something for himself and Rob, a pattern they'd fallen into since the summer holidays had started and Matt was at home.

'Did you know, Dad, Peter's going to be a veterinary nurse?'

Rob nodded. Peter had mentioned this was what he wanted to study at college.

'He's good wi' animals, that's for sure.'

Peter's face lit up, pleased by this praise. He pushed his hair behind his ears, tucking into another sandwich. He needed a good haircut. This seemed to be the preferred style of the young ones these days – long and untidy. Matt's was the same. Rob couldn't get him near a barber. He took after his mother, fair hair and pale skin, but it was his eyes that caught Rob out – he had Lorna's way of looking at you, as though trying to read your thoughts, his blue eyes intense.

Peter asked what needed done that afternoon. Rob's reservations about taking on a student had proved unfounded. What Peter lacked in experience he made up for in enthusiasm, always turning up on time each morning, working hard.

What was more, Matt was showing a greater interest in the farm. Rob would come into the milking parlour to find both Matt and Peter putting on the clusters, or they'd be cleaning out a shed together, one forking, the other wheeling away.

They were always talking when Rob came in for his lunch.

'Do you like the darkness?' Matt was asking Peter as Rob came through the kitchen doorway.

'Sure, it's still the summer,' said Rob, as he washed his hands at the sink. 'The nights are hardly dark at all.'

Matt and Peter burst out laughing.

'*The Darkness.*' Matt emphasised the words as though this would make Rob understand. 'We're talking about music!'

It was good to hear laughter in the house again, even at his expense.

Later that week, Rob moved the cows to a different field. He could have done with help, but the bull was with them. It was used to Rob; he knew how to handle it safely.

He had told Peter to fence any gaps in the farm hedges. Rob could hear the ring of hammer against steeple as he closed the gate on the cows. He walked across the fields in the direction of the noise to see how he was getting on. The hammering ceased as Rob got closer. Peter was standing still, the hammer hanging in his hand, looking down the hill towards the farmhouse.

Rob stopped when he realised what Peter was watching. Matt was hanging clothes on the line in the garden. He bent over the basket of washing, then reached up to peg the clothes, his T-shirt rising up his back. Peter's eyes never left him as he emptied the basket. Rob turned, walking back the way he had come.

He knew then, knew what was happening, wasn't stupid, but wouldn't let himself believe it. They had become good friends, that was all. He couldn't let himself think otherwise – the unthinkable.

The phone rang one day, a girl wanting to speak to Peter. 'Please, ask him to ring me. To ring Fiona.'

When they were eating lunch, Rob said, 'Fiona was on the phone.' Peter's face coloured. 'Ye didn't tell us ye had a girlfriend.'

The summer was almost over. Matt had got the exam grades needed to go back to do A levels, but to Rob's relief his son never mentioned it, getting stuck in every day on the farm.

Rob began leaving the milking to Matt and Peter while he got on with other jobs.

The sheep broke out of their field into a neighbour's farm. Rob headed back to the yard to get the boys' help.

No sign of them outside.

They were in the kitchen. There was a murmur of voices as Rob entered the house. The kitchen door was ajar. They stopped talking. Peter's back was to Rob. Matt stepped forward, his arms going around him, their lips meeting.

Rob was outside again.

Something inside his head was beating, getting faster, more insistent.

He found himself in the milking parlour. If he could only block it out, erase it from his mind. He walked down the parlour in slow, measured steps, trying to calm his breathing, trying to stop the pounding in his head.

A footstep behind him.

Peter's voice.

'Will I bring in the cows?' Peter repeated.

'I need ye to move the bull into the pen.'

The image of Matt played over and over in Rob's mind; his son's expression as he held another man in his arms. He had never seen such intensity of emotion in Matt's eyes, on his face . . .

The sound of yelling brought Rob to his senses.

What had he done?

He grabbed a stick, ran from the parlour, towards the other end of the yard.

Peter was slumped against the pen rails, the bull ramming into him. Rob shouted as he ran, tried to get the bull's attention.

He reached the pen, rushing at the bull, brandishing the stick.

It backed off.

Peter was face down on the ground. Rob lifted him under his arms, his hands slipping on the bloody clothes, dragging him out. He could hear Matt's screaming voice somewhere behind him. He had almost got Peter to the gate, but the bull was moving towards them . . .

Matt came through the hospital ward door.

His eyes were bloodshot. He tried to smile at his father. It pained Rob that he was so upset.

He sat on the chair beside the bed. Rob should ask about the funeral. Should say something to comfort his son. Sentences formed in his head, but he couldn't speak them. Didn't trust his voice not to give him away.

He had to keep hating Peter; the alternative was unthinkable, that Rob had caused another person's death without the justifiable reason that he was protecting his son. If only Lorna were here. None of this would have happened. She would have made Matt see the huge mistake he was making.

'Whatever he chooses, we have to support him.'

The realisation hit Rob with a jolt as he remembered her words, what she'd said after telling him their son wanted to be an accountant. She had meant more than his choice of career.

Matt was watching him with those serious blue eyes of his mother's. Rob couldn't bear to look at him. He turned away his head, but could never block it out – Matt and Peter in the kitchen.

'Dad . . .'

Rob reached out his hand towards his son. Matt's fingers were trembling. His father grasped his hand tighter, to make up for the consoling words he couldn't say.

'Fiona.' Matt's voice faltered. 'Fiona's outside.'

Rob frowned, didn't know anyone called—

'Peter's . . . girlfriend.'

Stringing the poor girl along, and at the same time corrupting his son. A piece of work that lad was, worst mistake Rob ever made, taking him on.

'She wants to thank you, for trying to save him.' Matt slowly shook his head. 'He knew not to go near the bull. I, I don't understand why . . .'

Rob had protected Matt; had acted in the best interest of his son. Peter was a piece of work.

'He was leaving.' Matt's lip quivered. 'He told me that day, the day he . . . He'd got a job on another farm. He was going to tell you, he said, after milking. I don't understand. The bull, why he would . . .'

Rob glanced at the ward clock. How much longer until visiting was over? The funeral had unleashed something in his son. He wasn't the silently grieving boy he had been before.

'I . . . begged him to stay.'

If Lorna were here, Rob knew she'd say, *We understand, Matt. We're fine about you being* . . . Rob couldn't think the word, never mind say it.

'He loved Fiona, you see.' Matt raked his hands through his hair, tears pouring down his face.

'He . . . wasn't like me. He thought he might be, but I, I shouldn't have tried to kiss him. Why would he have gone in with the bull, Dad? He knew not to. Must have been because of me. He was upset, not– not thinking straight.'

Tell him it was your fault. Lorna's voice in Rob's ear. *You can't let our son think he was responsible.*

Matt wiped his eyes on his sleeve. 'She's in the waiting room. Fiona.'

How are you going to live with yourself, Rob? The guilt will be unbearable. Say it was you not thinking straight, you told him to move the–

'She wants to thank you. For risking your life.'

Matt managed to smile at his father through his tears.

Rob tried to form the words, construct the sentences he needed to speak.

'She wants to meet the hero.'

Rev Ricky

*S*HE GLANCES BACK. *He's gainin' on her!*
Turns street corner, weavin' through dolls with prams
on pavement. Out me way! Out me way! Past chemist . . .
past bookies . . .

In shop windee sees he's right behind her.

Swerves down an alley.

Past a poster for The Com.

The Cross-Community Centre. 'The Com,' Rev Ricky calls it. Saturday night youth club – better than stuck with Ma and Himself in front of the telly, actin' like they've no legs, 'Get us more bevvies, Lan, there's a girl.'

Ping pong, darts, pool – crap like that. Tea and bickies, many's you want, 'stead of stuck in the house, Ma and Himself cosyin' up on the sofa.

The Com on the news: '*Leaders from Catholic and Protestant communities bringing young people together in a new initiative . . .*'

'Good on them,' says Ma. 'War's over. Hey Lan, you'll find

yerself a nice Proddy.' Ma and Himself near fallin' off the sofa laughin'.

Dog collar, badge – Reverend Richard Richardson. *Don't stare Lan*, Ma's voice in her head.

'And you are? . . . Lovely to meet you, Leanne.'

His voice. Like . . . music, poetry. Y'think some crap, Leanne!

Out other end of alley, his feet drummin' behind her. She's in a carpark, aul doll with a dog comin' towards her, one of them long leads, stupid mutt dashin' cross her path, gonna trip her up!

Leap, Leanne!

Won't get high 'nough!

Yes! Feet land down.

Thuddin' . . . shoutin'. She glances back. He's on the ground, lead wrapped round his legs. She'd laugh, if she'd any frickin' breath left . . . quick, quick, Leanne, this is yer chance to lose him.

There's visitors the night, come to The Com on a bus from the Shankill. They look frickin' terrified, as if expectin' to get their heads beat in.

Rev Ricky talks to her; he talks to everyone, Leanne! She's been practisin' no effin' or blindin'. Her throat's dry as toast; she's starin' at his chin, can't lookee him in the eye wi'out her cheeks burnin' up.

It's Rev Ricky's turn on stage; she's filmin' on her phone: 'As we mark the twenty-fifth anniversary of the Good Friday Agreement . . . integrating the schools is the only way to ensure lasting peace and stability in Northern Ireland . . .' She goes upta him after, has it all rehearsed. 'Must be hard like, bein' piggy in middle.' Rev Ricky smiles, nods; but knows he's thinkin', same's her – she's jus' called him a pig! Her face is on frickin' fire!

Across the car park . . . outta breath . . . hotel! Back entrance. Lookees over her shoulder, he's on his feet again, comin' after her . . .

Inside . . . stairs. Runnin' up them . . . corridor, doors each side – locked, locked. Next door – open!

Paint tins on floor, everythin' covered in sheets. No one there. She crawls under a dressin' table, arranges sheet again.

He's in the room! Hole in sheet, sees him! He goes inta bathroom . . . out again, lookees round . . . rips down a sheet, opens a wardrobe door –

'Hey! What you doin'!' Painter, tins in hands.

He scarpers.

What now? If only she'd her phone. Dropped it when he twigged she were there. Twig, ha, not funny, Leanne.

Painter swooshing paint on wall. Could say, 'Help me!' Don't trust no one, Leanne . . . She creeps out, tippytoes to door, lookees each way . . . Along corridor, heart goin' rackety-rack, peeps round corner . . .

No signs of him.

Lift!

Down, down. Glass doors, outside, street, pavement . . . walks, keeps head down . . . senses, glances back – run, Leanne, run!

Can't sleep. Plays Rev Ricky, phone close upta her face. The Com were on the telly again, '*Dissident groups appear determined to undermine . . . cannot be allowed to take us back to the dark days of the Troubles. We must stand united in solidarity, in prayer. . .'* Ma's eyes poppin' when she seen him on stage. 'That's why you're always down there, Lan,' bustin' herself laughin'.

Her belly's growlin', but can't chance goin' downstairs to kitchen. She plays Rev Ricky again 'stead. She could turn Prodes- Protestan- whatever the frickin' word is – would see Rev Ricky alls the time, ev'ry Mass.

Cars, vans, whizz, whizz . . . quick, quick, Leanne! She darts through . . . Horns! Tyres squeal!

She's at other side!

He's left behind. Ha! She sprints up pavement. Second wind.

Hold-handers, kiddies – out me way! Out me way! Gonna lose him this time. Hasta lose him . . .

A dog barks. She don't close the curtains, can see out windee from her bed, likes seein' the moon. Shines on rows and rows of houses, same's hers; rows and rows of back yards, same's hers. Someone's walkin' down the alley, what they doin' this time of night? They stops at door into yard opp'site. No one lives there, windees boarded up, why they goin' in there? They're liftin' somethin'. . .

Next mornin' she's forgot alls 'bout it. Ma says, 'Lan, take out the bin on yer way.' Himself never bothers; he's on early shift, least gets to eat brekkie just her and Ma. Wheels bin out to alley, lookees at door in wall inta yard opp'site.

A state, aul broke chairs, bags of rubbish. Stinks. *Coal bunkey?* Were that what someone were doin' last night, liftin' lid? *Nosey cow, keep yer neb out*, Ma's voice in her head.

Somethin' wrapped in a towel.

Throat sore, chest sore, pantin' . . . glances back. Can't run no more. He's right behind her. Not fair, can run faster!

Shop entrance. Swerves, stumbles . . . doorman catches her 'fore she falls. 'Woah, where's the fire?'

Tell him you've lost yer phone, Leanne, ask him to ring Ma; you can trust Ma. But what'll Ma do? She'll tell the coppers . . . 'You alright, love?' Doorman got a kind face. She's gonna gurn, hasta blink real hard.

Glances round, where is he? Mabe he didn't follow her in! Scans shop . . . sees him! Eyeballs her.

But he can't grab her here, not in Marksies.

She smiles at doorman; starts shoppin' . . . lookee there – cardi for Ma. She can't outrun him; think of other way to lose him . . . think, Leanne!

Hasta wait till Saturday night to tell Rev Ricky, been bustin' to tell all week, almost says, *Hey Ma*, but Rev Ricky always goin' on 'bout anyone needin' to talk 'bout anythin'. '*We must work together to protect and nurture our cherished peace.*' She taps his shoulder, tilts her head; he follows her over to a corner. She's it all practiced, 'bout seein' someone goin' inta the yard in the middle of night, the coal bunkey; but she's never been stood this close to Rev Ricky, could kiss him, stick one on him now, might be only chance she gets.

'What is it, Leanne?'

'I seen a gun.'

He's standin' next her . . . follows her along rail of cardis, keeps right behind her. She's gonna gurn . . . blink, blink, Leanne, don't let 'em out. How's she gonna lose him, will be right behind when she leaves shop – oh, lookee, over there!

'Excuse me, sir!' Posh voice. 'You can't come in here. This is a ladies' changing area!' She pulls cubi curtain, sits on stool, head down . . . quit frickin' gurnin', Leanne.

Rev Ricky frowns. 'Oh . . .' Alarm in his beautiful eyes; he's got real long lashes, longer than hers, longer than anyone's. 'Where did you see the . . . *it*, Leanne?'

'In yard. Not ours, someone else's.'

'A toy gun, Leanne? Plastic? They can look *very* realistic.'

She brings out her phone; his fingers touch hers as she hands it him, firecrackers pop- pop in her head!

Shocked, when sees pic. 'Leave it with me, Leanne.' Line like crater 'tween his eyes, and now she's thinkin', knows he's thinkin' too, what it says on the wall up road 'bout squealers – RATS WILL BE SHOT

Blood-red paint.

What now? Peeps round cubi curtain. He's standin' guard at entrance. Think, Leanne. Think! Lookee round – walls, pegs, mirror, stool. Lookee up . . . Stand on stool . . . not high 'nough to see over cubi!

Lyin' on her bed. Watchin'. A while 'go, seen Himself come back from pub. She's doin' survel– survelli . . . that thing they do in films, watchin' for the baddie. Rev Ricky'll be impressed.

She's gonna be a copper. First thing she'll do, arrest Himself, cuff him, no more his paws all over Ma – *Oh*, lookee, someone in the alley, goin' inta stinky yard . . . unwrappin' gun . . . puttin' in his jacket.

Small; black clothes. Remember details, Leanne! He walks back down alley, silver stripes on his black trainers glint in the moonlight; wink, wink, wink. A detective, that's what she's gonna be.

When he comes back with gun, she'll follow him.

She peeps round cubi curtain again. He's still on guard. Marksie woman there, givin' him the evil eye, says somethin' in posh cross voice. He walks a bit away.

Dashes out cubi . . . into next cubi, grabs stool, back inta hers.

Stools one top 'nother . . . climbs up . . . they falls over, she bangs her frickin' knee!

Lets herself outta the house, real quiet. Mustn't wake Ma or Himself. Real cold, crouchin' next fence, can peep through, see anyone goin' up alley. Dressed black; she'll take a selfie to show Rev Ricky, gets out phone – freezes! Someone comin' up alley . . . Winky trainers goes past! Creak of door inta stinky yard . . . Creak again . . . Wink, wink, past fence, past her hidin'.

She waits . . . follows.

He turns down a street.

Goes in a flat.

Lives jus' two streets from her.

Tries again. Stool on top other . . . Careful, careful . . . Yes! Can see over. Lookee – EMERGENCY EXIT! Stools start shakin', cling on Leanne, pull yerself over . . . You can do it! You can do it!
    Clambers over, drops down other side.
    Yes! Yes!

Saturday afternoon. Ma's gettin' her hair done. 'Give the carpets a goin' over, Lan, there's a girl.' Detectives don't hoover! She walks up road, needs somewhere to hide, to do survelli– survellilancy. Oh, lookee up ahead, someone's comin' out his street. Small, baseball cap. Lookee – silver stripe trainers. Half of town's got silver stripe trainers, Leanne! She'll follow him anyways. Practice!

Runnin'. Chest sore . . . hasta keep runnin'. Pictures him standin' in Marksies. Cubi's empty, she's not there! Ha, got one over on him! She'd laugh, if her lungs weren't frickin' bustin', if she weren't runnin' for her frickin' life . . .

Follows winky trainers to park.
    He sits on a bench. She walks past like detectives do on telly, circles back behind. He lookees up path; must be waitin' for someone!
    Bushes behind bench. She crawls under.
    Can't see him through the leaves, 'cept for his feet.
    Someone else's feet, beside his. Dirty white trainers, green and yella stains, no stripes. Gets out her phone, real quiet. Record what they say, Leanne. Evidence!
    Wait a minute. She knows them trainers . . .
    'Richardson, he's called.'

Himself's voice!

Almost drops her phone.

'The God Squad. Been down the station, says he's inf'ma-tion. Wants protection 'fore he squeals.'

Must be a baddie copper leaked this. Don't trust no one, Leanne!

'Do 'im the night.'

Leanne gasps. Clamps her hand over mouth.

They're not talkin' no more.

Holds her breath.

Winky trainers move. He musta heard her! Gonna come round bush, grab holda her! . . . Winky trainers walk away.

Himself sits on.

Why don't he frickin' walk away?

A spider, 'bout to climb her leg . . . *ugh!*

Moves her foot.

Loud snap.

A twig.

Dirty trainers move like light'ning.

She scrambles out from bush; drops phone.

Himself lunges at her, gets holda her sleeve.

She twists free.

Runs.

Home.

Ma . . . she wants her mammy! She's not here Leanne, you know she's at the frickin' hairdressers.

Get gun, Leanne!

Inta stinky yard.

Coal bunkey.

Puts it in her pocket.

Himself comin' up alley.

Run Leanne, other way up alley, get to The Com! To Rev Ricky!

Gonna make it . . .

She's near there . . .

Glances back.

He's gainin' on her.

Won't make it . . . Won't make it!

She stops.

Spins round.

Puts hand in her pocket.

He stops.

Smiles.

'C'mon Lan, you're not gonna shoot me, girl.'

Hand shakin'. Grip tighter. Gonna be a copper, Leanne. You can do this.

'What'll yer Ma think?'

'Stay back!'

'C'mon Lan, you're not really gonna . . .'

Pull trigger! No more his slimy paws alls over Ma, alls over her when Ma not there. Pull trigger!

'Leanne!'

Rev Ricky?

'Lower the gun, Leanne. I'll make a citizen's arrest.'

You wha'?

They wrestle.

Don't hurt Rev Ricky!

She points gun again.

What if she misses, what if she shoots Rev Ricky 'stead?

Crack!

Himself breaks free, legs it.

She lookees up at sky. You just shot a frickin' cloud, Leanne!

Rev Ricky's hands on hers. 'Give me the gun, Leanne.'

Her hand's stuck to it; he lifts away her fingers. Sets it real careful on the ground, steps slowly backways, as if not trustin' it to stay put.

Her legs all wobbly; coppers don't faint, Leanne!

Rev Ricky catches her in his arms.

She lookees inta his eyes; it's like one of them love films, then she remembers, 'What we gonna –'

'Shh,' says Rev Ricky. 'It'll be okay, Leanne.' Telling her what a brave girl she is, stroking her hair, knows she's picturin' the paint on the wall, blood-red, RATS WILL BE . . . she don't care though, 'cause she's in Rev Ricky's arms.

She'll dies happy.

The Portrait

MARLENE SITS AT the harbour during the tourist season, always at the same spot beside the railings. She clips a new page to her easel, her long, grey-threaded hair held back by a ribbon, which flutters in the breeze. People pause as they walk by, admiring the paintings on display.

She gazes at the view that she has painted for over thirty years. A yacht is pulling out of the marina to her right, into which visitors arrive during the summer in their grand vessels.

Her eyes follow the progress of the yacht across the harbour. A woman comes up on deck with a camera, her white trousers and red-striped top billowing, taking photographs of the cliffs bordering the other side of the harbour, with the row of fishermen's cottages along their foot. This is where Marlene lives, where in winter, waves crash almost to her door.

The yacht makes its way out of the harbour, and Marlene picks up her paintbrush. She will include it in her painting, a white fleck on the horizon where the sea merges into the brighter blue of skyline.

A young couple appear beside Marlene, lifting a painting

to study it closely. Marlene glances at them, and they smile at her. She sees the curiosity in their eyes, knows they have heard her story. They have heard about the fisherman's widow who paints at the harbour, whose husband was lost at sea many years ago, shortly after they were married. They will take note of her shabby clothes – the long black skirt with a ragged hem; the patched blouse. They will say afterwards how old-fashioned she dresses; how quaint she looks.

She has got used to being pitied. It is part of who she is, fitting her comfortably, like her faded clothes. It also helps to sell her paintings. She must earn enough during the summer to last through the long winter.

Marlene, like many others, needs the tourist trade which has grown over the years, but with it has come unwelcome changes to this quiet fishing harbour. Property developers want to buy her cottage. Houses along the bay have been demolished and holiday apartments built in their place. She was asked to name her price, but Marlene wasn't interested in their promise to make her a rich woman. Wealth goes hand in hand with evilness, she learnt that a long time ago.

Marlene wraps the painting for the young couple. They ask if she does portraits?

It is a quiet day, with just a few passers-by. The lack of inter-ruption means Marlene makes good progress on her painting, is so engrossed she doesn't realise at first that someone is stan-ding behind her.

'You do portraits?' The foreign voice of a tourist.

'You're the second to ask today,' Marlene replies, glancing at him as he steps forward.

It must be an illusion, her mind playing tricks.

Her husband is standing beside her.

He looks the same as the last time she saw him, over thirty years ago.

She turns her gaze back to her painting, anywhere but at him. The brush trembles between her fingers; somehow she continues its sweep over the page.

'I don't do portraits,' she says, and he stands a few moments more before walking away along the harbour, her eyes following him, his dark wavy hair lifting at his shoulders with the rise and fall of each stride.

Marlene packs up her things, hurriedly making her way home. The familiar swoosh of water breaking on the shore calms her slightly as she walks the coastal path, then the relief of closing and locking the cottage door behind her.

She lowers herself into a chair. The sea can still be heard, the lap of water against the rocks below her cottage. Marlene remembers the roar and crash of the waves on the night her husband didn't come back. The next day they found his boat, what was left of it, smashed on the rocks at Gidon Head.

They had not yet been married a year.

She had sat on this chair, day after day, looking out, willing the sea to return him so that she could have a grave to mourn at, to take flowers to. She could afford a proper headstone. This thought had brought her some comfort, and she had gone to the hiding place concealed in the cottage wall, taking out the box containing her inheritance, the money her family gave her when they washed their hands of her. She could marry a fisherman if she chose, but they would never see her again. The box was empty. How could the money be gone? No one else knew about it, or about the hiding place, except her husband.

Now, she gazes through the cottage window, knowing everything is about to change. She sits until the light fades, the waves outside whispering what she already knows.

Tomorrow, he will come back.

Marlene sets up her easel at the harbour. In the summer she never misses a day, and today is no exception.

She continues work on her painting. The sea is a different colour than yesterday; its tones constantly change. She adds a finishing touch – a white fleck on the horizon, which only she will know is the yacht she watched set sail the day before.

'They say your husband was lost at sea.'

His voice behind her.

Marlene clips a new sheet of paper to her easel. 'I told you yesterday, I don't do portraits.'

He doesn't move away, watches, as she begins a new painting. She wills her hand to stay steady, and it does, sweeping colour across the page. The sky is cloudless today, the expanse of sea stretching as far as she can see. The outcrop of rocks at Gidon Head is beyond her vision, even on a clear day like this.

He stays silent, standing behind her shoulder. She can hear his breathing. Her fingers holding the paintbrush are clammy; their strokes on the page start to falter.

A family pause to view her paintings.

The sound of his footfall walking away.

Marlene sits at the window of her cottage. Never tires of watching the sea, but tonight it is the huge crimson sun that transfixes her, slowly disappearing at the skyline, reflecting on the water, as if bleeding into the ocean's depths.

The candle on the table burns lower; shadows begin to flicker on the white-washed cottage walls.

The knock on the door startles her, even though she is expecting it.

His outline in the doorway makes her catch her breath. How many times had she hoped, prayed, for her husband to appear there.

His dark eyes hold hers.

'What do you want?'

'The cottage.' He looks past her into the dimly lit interior. 'It is mine.'

His face is so similar to the one she once loved.

'My father told me about it. It was his; now it is mine.'

Marlene opens the door wider for him to come in. She must try to appear calm.

'I can pay you what the cottage is worth,' Marlene says, 'if you will leave me in peace.'

His eyes are scornful. 'You don't know, do you, what this is worth? They will build many apartments here.'

'I will pay you,' Marlene repeats.

He shakes his head at her ridiculous words.

'Did your father not tell you about my family?' She has to stop herself from adding – Did he not tell you about my inheritance he stole?

'I have something very valuable. I will give it to you, and every penny I have, if you will leave me in peace.'

She goes into the back room of the cottage, returns with a box, offering it to him.

His thoughts are obvious in his eyes – *stupid old woman. What could she possibly have?*

Inside the box, on top of her savings, is a diamond brooch. The large stone glistens in the candlelight. It was part of Marlene's inheritance. She has always worn it, pinned to the lining of her skirt for safekeeping. Her husband's son studies it, a smile at the corner of his mouth.

'You will leave me in peace now,' Marlene says.

He pockets the brooch, glances at the few pieces of furniture in the cottage. 'You have until tomorrow to pack up your things.'

Marlene opens the drawer under the table.

Points the knife.

'What will you do with that?'

The knife trembles in her hand; she tries to hold it steady, to make him see she is serious.

'Go on, then.'

He laughs.

Her arm lowers.

He walks to the door.

Glances back; her husband glancing back, the last day she saw him, just a quick swivel of his head, same as now, before turning his back on her.

Marlene's fingers tighten on the knife handle, her feet move, rush of their own accord.

He cries out.

The box falls from his hands, the notes inside fluttering to the floor.

Marlene paints every day at the harbour during the tourist season.

Passers-by pause to admire her paintings. As well as seascapes, she has begun doing portraits – charcoal sketches, which are proving popular with visitors.

The young woman sitting for her today must have heard Marlene's story, heard about the attempted robbery of the widow's savings. Marlene sees the curiosity mingled with admiration in the woman's eyes.

Marlene's hand moves rapidly over the page. This skilful capturing of a person's face has easily come back to her.

When her husband's son lay cold on her cottage floor, she realised people would recognise him, that they would question her story. She had brought out the last sketch she had done, over thirty years ago. Her husband, on their wedding day. Marlene gazed at the portrait, at her husband's shoulder-length wavy hair and the gleam in his dark eyes, but that was where the similarity with his son ended. Their features – shape of nose, mouth, and chin – were very different. She didn't understand how they could have appeared identical to her.

The young woman is delighted with her portrait. She shows it to her brother. 'You have captured her spirit,' he says to Marlene.

They move away. Marlene gazes beyond her easel to the sea-filled scene before her. The morning mist has cleared. Her eyes sweep across the vastness of water to where, just beyond her vision, the rocks of Gidon Head jut from the mainland, at which many sailors have lost their lives, where her husband faked his death.

She will mark the rocks in her new painting, a tiny brown fleck only she will recognise, where the sea meets the sky. She puts her hand on her waist, tracing the outline of her brooch underneath her skirt.

It wasn't a physical resemblance to her husband that Marlene saw in his son.

She realises now.

It was the face of cunning she recognised – the portrait of a thief.

Memory Tap

SOMETHING NIGGLED AT the back of Max's mind; something was happening today. He gazed at the kitchen tap as he washed his breakfast dishes, trying to will it into his mind. He did this every morning, as if it were a memory tap, as if what he needed to remember would spout from it.

Lately, his memory had become a foreign land to him; somewhere on the horizon, just out of reach.

What could be happening today? It wasn't as if he had a full diary. In fact, he didn't keep one; what was the point when he had nothing much to write in it? Dee had kept a diary, filling each page with the smallest details. *Rained today, Bought new suit, Had headache.*

If Max had a dental appointment, for instance, he wrote it on the calendar, so he wouldn't forget, unless he forgot to look at the calendar, which was sometimes the case.

The tap wasn't stimulating any clues to the day's agenda.

Monday had an X through it on the calendar; had he done

that today or yesterday? It was either Monday or Tuesday. In the box for Tuesday he had written *Anne*.

If it *was* Tuesday, he needed to tidy up before she came. Although, the house was seldom untidy; Max couldn't abide clutter. Now that he lived alone it surprised him how easy it was to keep the place spic and span. Such a fuss women made about having to do housework.

Dee had been insulted by the label 'housewife'. If she had to write her occupation on a form she had groaned. She filled in DOGSBODY once, but it didn't seem to make any difference to what they were applying for. She had looked after him well, he had to admit that; the other chaps at the office hadn't had a crease like his in their shirt sleeves. Razor sharp. It had made him feel sharper, given him an edge.

He had complimented Dee often on her cooking; no one could accuse him of taking her for granted . . . although they had. Who was it? He could remember distinctly the words being said – *she deserved better than you* – but couldn't put a name to them. Perhaps, when he had got through all the books of puzzles Anne brought him, his memory would return from its holiday in distant climes. Each Tuesday, she came armed with crosswords and sudoku, as though problem-solving was the first line of defence against senility.

Anne was a housewife. He'd had such ambitions for his first-born child, but she seemed to relish her role as homemaker. He had wanted to call her Cassandra, but Dee thought it a pompous name. Dee liked short, sharp names, not Deirdre or Maxwell or Cassandra. Max had insisted on the 'e' at the end, instead of 'Ann'.

The doorbell rang.

That would be Anne.

She kissed him, their hug awkward as her hands were holding shopping bags. 'How are you, Dad?' she asked, speaking loudly, even though his hearing was perfect.

'Very well, thank you,' he said loudly back.

He looked into the bag she reached him, feigning interest in the crossword magazines inside.

In the other bag was a Tupperware container. Anne was a great baker; Dee had taught her well. He opened the lid. *Butterfly buns.* His eyes filled up; he had to blink rapidly. It was like smelling Dee's perfume.

Anne went over to the sink to fill the kettle. He brought out his handkerchief, wiping away the old man's tears on his cheeks.

'Where has everything gone? Where are all Mum's things?' Anne stared at the bare dresser, as if mesmerised by it, the same way Max had stared at the tap earlier.

She opened a kitchen cupboard; then another empty one. 'Where are all the cooking things? The blender, the mixer . . .'

'I didn't need all that stuff, so I took it . . .'

Where did he take it to? He had wrapped each item carefully in newspaper, putting them in boxes . . .

Dee had so many gadgets, odd-looking contraptions, he had no idea what they were for. It seemed like wizardry, or magic to him now, that she went to the shops and bought food, then transformed it through these various devices into wonderful meals. Not that he had taken her for granted; he had complimented her often on her culinary skills.

'Took it *where?*' said Anne. 'Don't say the charity shop!'

Max jolted his head up and down. Sometimes this helped jog his memory. He pictured his brain cells knocking into each other, wakening up.

Anne's hand flew to her mouth. 'How *could* you, Dad! They were antiques; Gran's mixer; the beautiful set of silver measuring cups; the Toby jugs . . .'

She put her hand on the slight curve of her stomach. 'I would have treasured them. I would have passed them on.'

'If it's a girl.'

A coldness in her eyes, reminding him of Dee. 'That's no longer relevant now they're gone.'

If Max *had* taken them to the charity shop – which he must have, because what else would he have done with them? – then he could get them back. *Buy* them back, if necessary.

Once Anne left, he found the number for the local charity shop in the Yellow Pages.

A recording.

They were closed on Mondays and Tuesdays.

He would try again tomorrow; wrote a reminder on the calendar.

Anne had set her Tupperware container of butterfly buns on the kitchen bench where Max could see them, instead of putting them into a cupboard. A statement, like the ones her mother used to make: *Here is the box of buns your loving daughter has baked for you, even though you don't deserve it.*

Dee would make a candlelit three-course dinner, not make eye contact with him, or speak, throughout the entire meal. *Here is the beautiful dinner your dutiful wife has made for you, even though you don't deserve it.*

Max had said to her, when the children were small, 'You

can always leave, you know. We could . . . separate.' Hadn't been able to bring himself to say 'divorce'.

'Is that what *you* want?' she replied.

'No! No, of course not.'

She had made a special effort after that; he could see the strain it put her under, forcing her face into a welcoming smile when he came home from work. 'Look, kids, Daddy's home!'

The forced jollity was worse than her coldness.

Max gazed at the kitchen tap as he washed his breakfast dishes . . . Maybe there wasn't anything he needed to remember about today.

Anne had visited yesterday, had brought butterfly buns. She had seemed annoyed with him when she left, not kissing him goodbye like she usually did. There were tears in her eyes; the pregnancy must be making her emotional. Dee had cried for days on end when she'd been carrying Fred.

On the calendar, Tuesday's box saying *Anne* was crossed off. In Wednesday's box it said *Charity Shop*.

Had he intended going to the charity shop today?

Were there things he wanted to take to it?

He jogged his head, once, twice, in quick succession.

Dee's clothes. That must be it! He'd been meaning to give them away; would have to face it, had been putting it off.

The wardrobe was crammed full. Dee loved fashion; Max had never complained about the amount she spent. He'd heard other men at the office grumbling about their wives' shopping sprees, but he'd liked Dee to look well. She'd always had a terrific figure, even after the children were born.

He took dresses off hangers, folding them in piles on the bed.

The doorbell rang.

Would be a door-to-door salesman. So many clothes! The doorbell kept on ringing. Max folded a lavender jacket and skirt, went downstairs.

'Hello, Dad.'

Had Fred arranged to come today? It wasn't on the calendar.

'Can I come in?'

They sat at the kitchen table.

Max cleared his throat. 'How's . . .' Fred had a wife and two sons; Max knew their names, but couldn't quite nail them down. '. . . everyone?'

Fred smiled. 'Fine, thanks.'

Ah, his mother's smile. But Dee had thought Fred took more after Max than her. 'Two peas in a pod,' she'd said.

'Anne phoned.'

Max looked over at the Tupperware box on the bench. 'She was here yesterday. Would you like a cup of tea?'

'She was talking about Mum's things.'

'Oh?'

Fred's eyes moved around the kitchen. 'The scales that used to be over there. The dresser china. The Toby jugs.'

Max had wrapped each item carefully in newspaper, packed them in boxes, then . . .

'You phoned last week, asked me to come over. Said you had stuff to take to the charity shop.'

Max gasped. Anne's face had been horrified, her hand moving to her stomach. '*I would have treasured them. I would have passed them on.*'

'It's okay, Dad. It's in my garage.'

Max breathed out with relief.

Another of his mother's smiles. Fred's hair was thick, brown and wavy, the way Max's once was.

'Alfred and Cassandra.'

Fred raised an eyebrow.

'What I wanted to call you, but your mother had to get her way.'

'She had great dress sense, hadn't she,' Max went on, 'a flair for putting outfits together. She always looked lovely, even in her apron, standing at the cooker, heavily pregnant with you. I wanted to tell her how lovely she looked.'

'Why didn't you?'

They hadn't been on speaking terms at the time.

'I'm clearing out her wardrobe.'

Max went over to the calendar after Fred left; he should ask Anne if she wanted any of her mother's clothes, would need a reminder so he wouldn't forget.

Underneath *Anne* in next Tuesday's box, he wrote *Dee's clothes.*

Anne's Tupperware box was on the bench. Max wasn't hungry; his appetite seemed to have left him these days, gone on holiday along with his memory.

He opened the box lid, closing his eyes as the aroma rose.

Dee's clothes wouldn't fit Anne at the moment, now that she was pregnant.

Why had he confessed to Dee when she was expecting? His timing couldn't have been worse. He shouldn't have told her. She would never have found out. Everything would have been different; their whole lives would have been different.

He'd thought she would forgive him. It had lasted only a week. 'A secretary,' Dee had said. 'Could you not be more original?' He had been relieved she was making a joke of it; then he saw the chill in her eyes.

She *would* forgive him, he'd told himself. It would take time, that was all. Anne was starting school. Fred was on the way; they had so much to look forward to. If it had been the other way round, he would have forgiven her. He wouldn't have wrecked their marriage over a brief affair.

What had possessed him to confess? He could have lived with the guilt, anything was better than her aloofness. She would forget and smile at him, her eyes full of warmth, and he would let himself hope, but it never lasted. She had called him unoriginal, but she was hardly original herself. *'Good day at the office, dear? Have you checked your collar for lipstick?'*

Max went back upstairs, carefully laid Dee's things flat in bags, not to crease them. 'Don't clear out her wardrobe, it will only upset you,' Fred had said, but there would never be a good time to give away her clothes. Max was glad someone else would get to wear such lovely fabrics – tweed and silk and velvet. Their new owner wouldn't suit them as well as Dee had. They wouldn't have her style, her way of putting an outfit together.

He filled the last bag, setting it beside the door with the others. Took out his handkerchief, wiped his eyes, blew his nose. Everything seemed to set him off these days.

Dee had moved into the spare room when she was expecting Fred. She told Anne an elaborate story, how she kept

Max awake with her tossing and turning: '*Daddy needs to be bright-eyed and bushy-tailed for work.*'

She never came back to their bed. A few afternoons with another woman, the rest of your married life without your wife beside you.

Didn't seem to balance out.

A Post-it Note on the kitchen tap:

Fred taking Dee's clothes to charity shop. Bring down bags from spare room.

The doorbell rang.

'Hello, Dad.'

A young, fresh-faced 'Max' on the doorstep.

'Are you okay?'

Max turned away, so his son wouldn't see his eyes filling up.

The car was crammed full by the time they got all the bags in.

'Did you ask Anne if she . . . ?'

Max didn't know what he was talking about.

'Just as well,' muttered Fred, '. . . big garage.'

'Pardon?'

'See you later, Dad.'

The kitchen was nice and tidy, with no clutter anywhere, except for the Tupperware box on the bench. Like a statement, but why was Max thinking that? It was just Anne's Tupperware box. Fred had said there was something he should ask her . . .

He jolted his head, once, twice.

Maybe, it was about the baby. She was very emotional now that she was pregnant; there had been tears in her eyes when she was here last. She needed her mother at a time like this; Max couldn't take Dee's place, but would be as supportive as he could.

He would buy baby clothes for the next time she was here! A nice surprise for her. What colour? He should know what Anne's favourite colour was . . .

He gazed at the kitchen tap for inspiration. The tiles behind it gleamed. Green would suit a boy or a girl.

Better write it on the calendar before he forgot. On next Tuesday's box it said *Anne.* Underneath: *Dee's clothes.*

What did that mean?

He scored out *Dee,* writing *Baby* beside *clothes* instead.

The doorbell rang.

Would be someone wanting to sell him life insurance, or new windows.

The woman on the doorstep had her back to him. There was something familiar about her hair, not the colour or style, but the springiness of it, the way it looked so alive.

She turned around.

Her face and neck were deeply tanned. Maybe, she was brown all over. What a strange thought to have! She was old; her face and neck lined. He was forgetting he was old too.

'Hello, Max.'

He put a hand on the door frame to steady himself.

'Can I come in?'

When Dee told him she was leaving, she had claimed it was Max who'd suggested it. '*You* said *we could separate.*'

That was back when the children were small!

Dee's sister lived in Australia; she'd always wanted Dee to visit (for both she and Max to go over there when he retired).

'Such wonderful news about Anne.'

'Is,' Max's words stuck in his throat, 'that why you've come back?'

Her fingers unknotted the silk scarf tied at the side of her neck. She looked wonderful. Suited her tan, her red hair.

She gazed around the kitchen. 'You've had a clear out.'

'I didn't think you were coming back.'

'It's only been a few months.'

How could it be . . . ? Had felt like years!

'I didn't deserve you,' Max blurted.

They were his words, had said them to himself. *You can't blame her for leaving; she deserved better than you.*

She re-knotted her scarf. Was going to leave again!

'Please don't go, Dee. The spare room is just as you left it. You don't even have to speak to me, as long as you stay. *Please.*'

The sound of the wardrobe door closing through the wall. The flick of the light being switched off. She would be getting under the covers . . . a creak from the spare room bed.

How long had she been back? Max had stopped crossing off the days on the calendar. He didn't need to; Dee was here again to keep him right. '*You've a dental appointment this morning, Max,*' or, '*Anne can't make it today, she's coming on Thursday instead.*'

The shade of her skin could be a clue to how long she'd been back. Her tan was long gone. The colour of her hair had stayed the same; Anne had hinted it was too young for her, but Max didn't agree. When you had Dee's style, you could carry off anything.

He closed his eyes. The sooner he fell asleep, the sooner tomorrow would come and he would see her again.

She had said, 'You didn't have to tell me about . . . All men are deceivers, according to my sister. At least you were honest.'

Max heard a noise; knew he must have fallen asleep, he'd had this dream before, in which the bedroom door clicked open, Dee's feet padded across the floor, and she got in beside him.

Something cold touched his foot.

His eyes shot open.

Dee's head was on the pillow beside his.

He lay absolutely still, afraid if he made any movement she would leap up. Her foot against his was freezing. Tears poured down his cheeks. He had to stop doing this. Even Anne's baby didn't cry this much. A smile spread across his face – Cassandra.

No doubt, downstairs, on the calendar, was a date marked, Cass's christening. Max was the only one who used her proper name, but he didn't mind, as long as his foot was warming Dee's cold one, her breaths deepening as she fell asleep beside him.

Max slept late the next morning.

Dee was no longer there; had he dreamt it?

The indent of where her head had been on the pillow.

He came downstairs.

Dee was in the kitchen. He had to blink rapidly. She looked so lovely, standing at the cooker.

She set his plate of bacon and eggs on the table.

'Who is "S"?'

His mouth was full. He swallowed. 'Pardon?'

Dee pointed to the calendar. 'It says on the first of November, "S," and underneath, "Birthday".'

Max didn't know. She must have written it.

'It's *your* handwriting.'

Max tried to think of anyone he knew with a name beginning with that initial.

Dee went out of the room, patted his shoulder on the way past, said she was nipping to the shop.

Max washed his breakfast dishes.

Gazed at the kitchen tap.

'*S*'?

Secretary – the word jumped into his mind. Why would he think that?

Siobhan.

How could he forget such a beautiful name?

His daughter.

The product of his brief affair with . . . He jolted his head up and down . . . How could he not remember her name?

His secretary.

Siobhan's mother.

He had given her money, for her and the baby, for the first few years, until she married, when she said she didn't want Max's support anymore. He had seen Siobhan just once, a few days after she was born. Her mother didn't want Max in her daughter's life, said her husband was now Siobhan's daddy. Max should have been relieved. Dee hadn't forgiven him yet about the affair. He had Anne and Fred. Had told himself it was best for Siobhan; she deserved better than him.

'They all deserved better than you,' he said out loud.

He had always thought about her over the years, Siobhan. The one time he'd seen her – wispy dark baby hair. It would have grown long, thick and wavy. She could have children of her own by now.

Max's grandchildren.

He got out his hanky.

Had been such a burden to carry, his secret child.

He had almost told Dee, about Siobhan, when she was born, had almost blurted, but knew he had to wait until she forgave him for the affair.

It was different now. Dee had come back from . . . a foreign country, because – he gazed at the tap again – because he'd been honest about the affair, that was what she had said!

He would tell her.

What if she left again? Went back to . . . the foreign place her sister lived.

He couldn't carry the burden of guilt any longer.

She would forgive him.

He had to tell her.

Needed to write a reminder, so he wouldn't forget.

A Post-it Note on the kitchen tap:

Tell Dee your secretary had a baby.

The Stole

CATHERINE SAT BESIDE Albert in the pew.

On her other side, Catherine's mother had a handkerchief under her veil, dabbing at her eyes. Catherine put a hand on her arm, squeezed it to say she understood this was for appearance's sake, knew she must be thinking, with immense relief, same as her daughter: *This is the last time I will be in his presence.*

Tears trickled down her mother's cheeks. She was genuinely upset. Catherine retracted her hand, faced straight ahead again at the coffin. She smiled behind her veil; soon he would be put into the ground.

Afterwards, in the carriage; the ring of hooves on the road; her mother's snuffling. *Like the pigs at home*, thought Catherine, *rooting for food amongst the trees.* She knew she was being unkind, turned her attention to Albert, wondering what thoughts were in his head as he gazed through the carriage window, her eyes lingering on his scar.

Catherine was the first to be seated at the dining table, exchanging a few words with Milly.

'What is the meaning of this?'

Catherine gave a start. The maid also jumped at Albert's raised voice behind them. 'Beg– beg pardon, sir.' Moving cutlery and glasses under his instruction to the head of the table, almost dropping the china in her haste.

Albert lowered himself into their father's wingback chair, looked down at Milly's handiwork. He laced his fingers, placing his chin on them, raised his gaze to his sister.

'Why?'

Catherine frowned, didn't know what he was referring to.

His lips stretched into a smile, imitating hers earlier.

'You know why,' almost burst from Catherine, but her mother's unexpected grief, and now the hardness in Albert's eyes, silenced her.

'Poor little Catherine has lost her tongue.'

'Little', as if she were still a child, instead of almost fifteen.

'I . . .' she began, struggling to put into words how she felt about their father, especially after. . . But it was never spoken of, just Albert's scar a constant reminder that her beloved brother, who had been her best friend, whom she used to laugh and play with, had become a stranger.

'I'm glad he's dead and so are you,' she said in a rush, suddenly angry, tears prickling at the back of her eyes; she'd been foolish to think Albert would come back to her, be his old self again.

Not only did Albert claim their father's chair, Catherine watched with disbelief as the latter seemed to rise from the grave and begin walking in Albert's shoes. The servants noticed the change in him as well. Catherine could see their hesitation, hear it in their voices as they tried to please someone who was not to be pleased.

A silence enveloped the house, as if everyone were holding their breath to see if this was a passing phase for Albert, an adjustment at the age of sixteen to becoming master of the estate. Catherine tried to put herself in his shoes, to excuse his sharpness and impatience. *Such responsibility he has now, he's just becoming accustomed to it.*

It became apparent that it wasn't a phase. He could deceive himself and everyone else, believing this was his true personality coming through, but Catherine knew better. Wouldn't, *couldn't* let herself believe it. He had never been fussy about his food; now not one course was to his liking. He set down his soup spoon. 'It's cold.' Milly rushed to lift it away, apologising.

Catherine put her hands around her bowl, not letting Milly take it. Across the table her mother's spoon froze, halfway raised, her eyes wide and shocked, which wasn't surprising to Catherine, as she now deferred to her son, as she had to her husband.

Catherine picked up her spoon.

'Take it all away!'

Poor Milly was scarlet, her hands trembling as again she went to lift away the bowl; for her sake Catherine almost let her do it.

Albert's eyes bored into the side of his sister's face.

He was on his feet, the bowl of soup crashing to the floor, Catherine's glass also being knocked over.

'Don't, Milly, you'll cut yourself.' But Catherine's words

were too late, she was already on her knees, gathering the broken china and glass into her apron. A tear dripped from the maid's chin. Catherine turned to Albert. *He looks in a trance.* His blank eyes fixed on Milly, the scarring on his temple silvery white compared to rest of his face, which had darkened in the summer weather.

Milly scurried away, clutching her apron in a bundle in front of her.

When the fish course was brought, their mother picked at the opaque flesh. *Am I to be weak like her?* The thought made Catherine hot with discomfort. *To accept this is how things will be . . .*

'Why do you no longer go shooting, Albert?' Catherine asked, willing her voice to sound calm and composed.

He continued eating, as though she hadn't spoken.

'Father would be disappointed.' A nerve jumped in his neck. 'The day Father first took you shooting . . .'

Albert stood abruptly, his knife and fork clattering onto his plate. Catherine wanted this, to see his temper flare at the right person.

Her mother watched him leave the room, her face ashen, eyes tear-filled; they had both lost him, the twelve-year-old boy who had changed overnight, becoming distant and silent. Had overheard her father: 'You and the girl have made him a weakling. Time he was a man.'

Catherine rose from the table, walked through the entrance hall, past the family portraits. Paused at the one of her father she usually avoided looking at, her heart beating quickly at the thought of what she was about to do. *I shan't let you win*, the thought giving her courage, a smile coming to her lips at the roll of fat under his chin. *Worms will feast well on that.*

She opened the front door, avoiding the quicker route through the kitchen, avoiding the servants, around the side of the house, along the path to the shed where they were stored, hung from a beam, and she almost wished the hooks had been empty, but there were two of them. She couldn't let the smell deter her.

Albert was in the library. She slipped in quietly, crossed the room towards him at the desk.

He raised his head, leapt up from his chair, backing away, his eyes wild. 'What . . . what are you . . . stay, stay away from me!' Catherine moved closer, the stink of its flesh unbearable to her now, as was the feel of the fur, a grotesque stole around her neck.

Albert backed into the corner of the room, his head down, looking anywhere but at her, yelling to leave him alone.

'He made you kill it, didn't he? *Father* made you.' She spat out the word.

He covered his face with his hands.

'It wasn't a clean kill, like this one.'

He wouldn't look at her.

'I wish it had been me, that I could have taken your place . . .'

Albert raised his head. His eyes were glazed; Catherine knew he didn't see her. 'Shot . . . it was shot in the leg. I– I pleaded with him to let it go, but he laughed, he– he took out his knife, told . . . told me to slit its throat, tried to force me, but the knife . . . the knife.'

Catherine's eyes moved to his scar.

'"It's just a scrape," he said, "stop blubbering like a girl."'

He . . . he put a rock in my hand, closed his fist over mine . . . pounded it– its . . .'

'I saw you.'

Shock in Albert's eyes.

'From my bedroom window. I saw you coming home. I thought *you* had been shot because of the blood . . . Then I saw it, saw the rabbit tied around your neck.'

His eyes filled with horror, and Catherine realised that he couldn't bear for anyone to have seen him that day. Instead of making things better she was making them worse.

She stepped closer to him, stretched out her hands, the hideous stole swinging, 'I was only trying to . . . I'm so sorry, can you forgive–'

He roughly pushed her away. *Now I have lost him forever* rushed through her mind as she fell, as her head hit the edge of a bookcase.

There was someone in the room with her; she knew this, even though she was asleep, and she knew it wasn't Albert because they were always there, knew that only her mother would stay with her day and night. Or Milly had been instructed to sit with her.

She didn't want to waken up because it wasn't Albert.

They never spoke, this person always by her side. *Or maybe I can't hear them*, the thought came to Catherine, and yet she heard voices in her dreams . . .

'*Cathy?*' Albert's voice, and she knew she must be dreaming again. They were in the garden, playing hide and seek. He was searching for her, under every bush, behind every tree.

'I'm here,' her lips moved silently.
Her eyelids flickered.
Opened.
In the chair beside her, he startled.
His cheeks were wet.
Her temple throbbed.
She smiled, despite the pain.
We shall have matching scars.

Flick the Slick

HAT THE!
Frank Saunders, of all people, opened the
door.

I recognised him straight off. It took him a mo. '*Flick?*'

His eyes travelled down me paint-spattered boiler suit. '*You're* the painter?'

His missus had phoned, hadn't give a name, just the road and house number.

'D'you wanna show me what needs doin'?'

He kept glancing sideways at me as we walked round the outside of his house. Mock Tudor, three stories. Would be worth a mint. Course he'd the toys to match, a Merc and a Jag on the driveway.

'Could fit you in next week, mate, if it stays dry.'

He burst out laughing, clapped me on the back. 'Okay, joke's over, Flick. Stop winding me up.'

There were times I couldn't get me head round it neither. Would hit me all of a sudden, when I were up a ladder scraping sills, or on me knees varnishing skirting. Flick the Slick, mastermind of the biggest and best cons, now had an ad in Yellow Pages – Colin Flickerton, painter and decorator.

Saunders followed me over to the van, put his big mug in the window. 'We could do a bit of business, Flick. You know, like the old days.'

When I didn't turn up to paint, he phoned. 'I've a guy here doing the house, but I've other jobs need doing, well-paid ones.'

I held out for most of a month. Were worse, the crick in me neck from rollering ceilings. I papered an entire downstairs, the customer weren't happy, the ole bat pointed out lumps. Had to take it off, pay for the new rolls from me own pocket.

I found meself outside Saunders's house. This time his missus answered the bell. A dolly bird, half his age.

'Flick!' Saunders appeared behind her.

He took me into his study. Shelves of expensive-looking books lined the walls. Saunders, a *reader*?

'So, what have you been doing?' His face spread into a smile. 'Apart from painting?'

'Wallpaperin'.'

He laughed, leaned back in his chair, the leather protesting, shook his head. 'C'mon Flick, serious now. I've something coming up might interest you.'

I almost replied, 'Nothin' you could say would interest me,' but why else were I here?

It were foolproof. Not that he said the actual words, but that were what he meant. He gave details – arrival of stock . . . switching packages . . .

I caught meself on. *Remember why you're retired! That job were 'foolproof'.*

'Not me thing, mate.'

I stood.

'A grand,' said Saunders.

I walked to the door.

'Two.'

Opened the door.

'Name your price.'

I kept a poker face. 'Five.'

He held out his hand.

It were just *one* job. I needed the cash to fix the van; took forever to start in the morning. *One* job, then back into retirement. Just had to create a distraction, keep the depot staff outta the way, while the packages got switched.

I couldn't concentrate, missed bits when I were painting, held the steamer on too long stripping wallpaper, cracked the plaster. I'd forgotten how it felt to have a hit coming up – dry mouth, crazy racing of your pulse when you thought 'bout it.

Unable to sleep. *Why's he giving you that kinda money for a distraction? Want another stretch, do you, Flick? Want another slow wink on your first day inside?*

The van were about to give up the ghost.

We'd arranged for Saunders to give me a grand up front the night before the job. His missus showed me into his study. She tossed her head, showing off her long blonde hair, gave me the eye.

Saunders's chair swivelled.

'All set, Flick?'

We'd made the arrangements. I had me clobber, me way in, would start the fire in a bin when I got the signal. Once the building were evacuated there'd be ten minutes, fifteen at most, to do the switch. I didn't know what the stock were; didn't want to know.

He reached me an envelope. 'The rest on completion.'

Unlocked a drawer, brought something out.

What the!

Set it on the desk between us. 'A precaution.'

He slid the gun towards me.

I focused on looking calm, shook me head.

'You're sorted then?'

I nodded. Course I had me own piece.

His booming voice rang out as I left, 'Like old times, eh Flick!'

One job, that were all. Weren't like I were going back to me former career. By this time tomorrow it'd be over. I pulled up at the side of the road, checked the envelope contained a grand.

Held a fifty quid note up to the light.

That were the thing about working with tricksters.

You couldn't trust them.

Me mobile rang the next morning.

Saunders.

'On me way, mate—'

'No, wait,' Saunders cut in. 'Change of plan. Come to mine.'

He opened the front door as I pulled up outside his house, hurried over.

I put down the window. 'What's up?'

'Have to postpone.' He were real annoyed. 'Must have got a tip-off. You wouldn't get near the place; it's crawling with security.'

I looked shocked.

His eyes bored into me, I knew he were thinking – *can I trust Flick? He's got me thousand quid. Were it him grassed?*

I thumped the steering wheel, let out a few expletives. 'So, what now?'

'Wait, I s'pose.' He sighed. 'So, tell us Flick, what else have you on?'

He big mug moved further in the van window.

'C'mon, spill. What you got coming up?'

Me paint-spattered boiler suit were rolled up on the passenger seat. 'This and that.'

Couldn't resist adding, 'Actually, somethin' real big.'

'C'mon, Flick, let us in on it! Work well together, you and me. You know that!'

I pictured him up a ladder next mine, in his collar and tie, painting the four-storey apartment block. I shook me head. 'Not your thing, mate.'

His mouth downturned. 'Will be in touch. The grand's just a deposit, mind, till the job's done.'

I fired the engine.

'C'mon Flick, cut me in on what you've on.'

'That guy you got to paint your house. He's missed a bit.' I pointed. 'See, next the garage.'

Saunders stepped back, looked over.

I were gone.

Without fail, the van started first time. Garage had sorted her. I patted the dash, gave her a good rev.

Me mobile rang.

Saunders.

A voicemail. 'Mine. Seven tonight.' Wouldn't go . . . but didn't want him turning up at the flat. The landlord kept promising to fix the broke window, do something about the damp.

Saunders's missus answered the bell.

Had overloaded on fake tan.

A smile; dimples; boob tube; short shorts.

'Boss in?'

She showed me into Saunders's office.

Indicated to take a seat.

Did I want anything? she asked, a twitch of her eyebrow – to drink or otherwise. Leant a bronze hip against the desk. I were eye level with a bare midriff, a sparkly belly hoop; she'd get a chill in her kidneys dressed like that, as me ole ma used to say.

I shook me head. 'No, I'm alright, mate.'

A smouldering look back as she closed the door behind her.

The wall of books had a gap.

Were fake; the fronts joined together, nothing behind. Typical.

Would tell Saunders I'd repay the grand so much a month . . . would take forever. *Better than being done for arson, Flick, anything better than doing another stretch. Remember you're irresistible not just to the ladies.*

Saunders came through the door.

Just the sight of him made me tense up.

'So,' he rested his forearms on the desk, steepling his fingers. 'Afraid it's a no go, Flick. The tip-offs put the wind up them. They've kept the increased security.'

Me muscles relaxed. Could almost hear them sigh.

I shook me head. Sombre-faced. Shame.

'But lucky for you I'm in need of a painter!'

I returned his smile.

Saunders chuckled. 'You've already got the clobber.'

Me smile froze.

'An adjoining house,' he explained. It was empty, up for sale. 'A painter there at the moment, but we'll get you in. Let's just say he won't be able to continue.' I pictured a ladder toppling; Saunders always were heavy handed. He brought keys out of his pocket. A trickle of sweat ran down me back, was like I could see the gun through the desk wood.

He opened a different drawer.

'No one in during the day.'

Chill, I told meself, as he slid equipment across the desk, gave more details. *Planting a camera, easy-peasy, done it many a time.*

Got outta the office before he could say, 'Like old . . .'

Looked in the mirror before leaving the flat. White boiler suit. Pretending to be meself. You couldn't make it up.

Row of ole houses, posh architraves, stained glass front doors. Done a bit of painting first, to settle the nerves. Kept a look out next door, in case someone showed.

Up me ladder to a back window, shimmied along the

sill, onto next door's trellis, a scary mo when thought it were gonna give! Down onto next door's balcony, picked the lock . . . put the camera on a light fitting.

Back to painting. Were finishing when I heard a vehicle pull up next door – might get a glimpse of the mark! Went over to the window. A classy bird got outta a car. Looked 'bout thirty; a suit, high heels, legs up to her chin.

That night, went back to Saunders's.

'Sorted then, Flick?'

I waited for him to put his hand inside his jacket, bring out a wad of big ones.

'Will be in touch. About step two.'

Which turned out to be blackmail.

Course. Why else plant a camera in a bedroom!

Saunders slid a folder across the desk.

Wouldn't mind seeing the classy bird with her kit off, but she were under the covers. First pic were of a bloke getting in beside her. *Hold on*, he looked kinda familiar . . .

Saunders were smirking.

I'd seen him, on the telly. Always wore a tie pin and double-breasted suit.

Couldn't be . . .

Saunders nodded.

What the?

Oliver Harrington.

The foreign – wait for it – secretary!

The classy bird worked for the council. I made an appointment. Dusted down the ole weddings-and-funerals suit, got out the Brylcreem. Looked in the mirror. Turned one way, then the other. *That's the ticket, Flick!*

Went round Saunders's. Mrs S. practically swooned when she answered the door.

'Alright, love?' Gave her a wink, which in hindsight were a mistake. But how were I to know she were a looney?

Saunders had a burner for me.

She were even more classy up close, covered head to toe, high-neck top, trouser suit, could teach Mrs S. a thing or two, leave it to the imagination. On the blower, I'd told her I were from a tenants' association, a landlord wouldn't fix the damp in his flats, cracked windows, and so on. Put the folder on her desk. 'Took some pics, so you'll get me drift.'

Me burner rang that night. *Him*, same posh voice as on the telly. I told him how much; she'd to make the drop. Where and when. Exchange for pics. A sarcastic laugh. 'No copies or hard drive?' 'Nope. Give you me word.' 'Why would I take you at your word?' ''Fraid you'll have to trust me on that one, mate.'

Were a hell of a lot of cash to get your hands on at short notice; according to Saunders, his father were minted, Lord Something-or-Other.

Did the pickup. Gave her the pics. Classy looked in pieces, wanted to put me arm round her and say, *Some advice, love – married men, real bad news.*

Back inta the van, up the road; stopped, checked the

readies. Too easy, made me twitchy, the job that got me banged up had been too easy.

Back to the big man's. This were it. I'd get me 4K!

Never have to see Saunders's ugly mug again.

I set the holdall on his desk.

He unzipped it.

The door flew open.

Mrs S., holding the gun.

'Take it easy, sweetheart,' Saunders told her in a soft voice.

'Don't *sweetheart* me, you . . .' and she called him everything under the sun, and then some. Were out of breath when she finished. She grabbed the holdall, indicated for me to move to the door. Saunders made a lunge for the gun.

It went off.

One of the fake books got it through the spine.

'Its cover's blew,' I quipped, trying to lighten the mood.

Mrs S. pushed me towards the office door, the gun trained on Saunders; locked it behind us. Pointed the gun at me. 'Move it. Hurry up!' I had to run with her to the van. For once I wished it wouldn't start, that Saunders would appear and wrestle her to the ground, but course it did, first time.

Up the road.

'Where to?' I asked.

'Airport.'

She kept the gun on me as we drove.

'They ain't gonna let you on a plane with a bag of cash, love. Where you gonna say you got all them smackeroos?' She frowned; hadn't thought of that. 'Need a plan,' I said. 'We'll pull over. Think it out.'

I stopped, cut the engine. Turned me head to her, looked deep into her eyes (pictured Classy), moved me head close; she moved hers close.

She were the most awful kisser, bit me lip, probably on purpose. I slid me hand up her leg. She were holding the gun on her lap. 'What, you're gonna keep hold of that? We're partners now, babes.' She smiled, her tongue darting over her teeth, like some kinda crazy lizard. I put me hand on hers holding the gun, 'Let's set it on the dash,' me other hand sliding further up her thigh.

She sighed, let me take the gun.

I hit her on the head with the butt. Hoped me ole ma weren't looking down through the Pearly Gates at that precise mo.

She slumped 'gainst the passenger door.

What now, Flick?

Think!

I got outta the van, round to her side, got her outta the passenger seat, round the back of the van, and into it. Bound her hands and feet. Probably weren't a listed use for masking tape.

Drove back towards Saunders's. *I know, Ma, don't look at me like that. She'd a gun on me! What were I meant to do?*

Shouting. Screaming.

What the!

Had to stop at traffic lights; the driver next me gawping

at the van. 'Help! Kidnap! I'm a hostage!' I took off like a bat
outta hell when the lights changed.

Turned onto a side road.

Inta the back of the van.

Gagged her.

I were almost out of tape.

Onto the dual carriageway again.

Not far now, to Saunders's.

A siren behind.

Flashing blue lights.

The Ole Bill! Wanting me to pull over!

The bloke at the traffic lights must've . . .

Had to stop; put down the window.

He took a good gawk at me. At inside of the van.

The holdall were on the passenger seat; were like it were
see-through – like he could see the gun and cash!

'Please, step out of the vehicle, sir.'

Asked me to follow him to the back of the van. I could
barely walk – blackmail, extortion, abduction, possession of
a firearm – they'd throw away the key.

'Are you *aware* you're breaking the law?'

A joker. Understatement of the year! Me legs were jelly,
me bowels about to give.

Waited for him to open the back of the van, start the
list . . .

'Are you aware, sir, that driving with a broken tail light
is illegal?'

Promised to get it sorted right away. Back onto the road, me knees knocking together. Getting the disapproving eye again. *I know, Ma, can't treat a lady like that . . . though she ain't exactly a– okay . . . okay!*

I pulled over, got out, round the back of the van; went to take the tape off her wrists; didn't trust her, were still that crazy look in her eye. '*Colin! No son of mine would . . .*' I started peeling, patted the gun in me pocket, don't be trying anything mind.

Back to Saunders's.

He came hurrying out of the house as the van pulled up.

I spread me hands. 'She done a runner.'

'*And the?*'

Shook me head.

He looked more upset about the money being gone than his missus. Started ranting 'bout how sly women were; underhand, sleeked and conniving . . .

'You'll square me up then, mate?'

'Kick a man when he's down, why don't you, Flick.'

'Weren't me fault! I done the pickup, brought it to you.'

'There's another job coming up.'

'We shook on it, Saunders.'

'C'mon Flick, cut me some slack.'

I put the van in gear. 'Don't never be in touch again, you hear!'

Drove down the driveway.

Wondered where Mrs S. were now? Knowing her, she'd

be trying to get through airport security with hundred quid notes stuffed down her bra.

When I took the tape off her mouth, she didn't hold it 'gainst me, knocking her out, wanted her and me to be an item.

'Sorry, already have a bird. Love of me life. Class act, so she is.' Told her as consolation she could have some of the readies.

'And the gun,' she said.

Blew me a kiss when I dropped her at the airport.

I chucked the gun in a river on the way back to Saunders's.

The holdall were in the back of the van.

In the rear-view mirror, the big man were watching me drive away.

No doubt Saunders had done *me* over in the past.

That were the thing about working with tricksters.

You couldn't trust them.

Bobby Dazzler

I T HAD ARRIVED.

Dull and overcast.

Michael gazed through the window at the grey sky.

His mum appeared beside him. 'Looks like rain.'

He tried to guess how she was feeling. She had encouraged him to agree to this. Did she feel differently now it was the actual day?

'Thought we'd leave about ten,' she went on, her voice matter-of-fact.

During his sleepless night, Michael had made a decision. 'I want to go on my own.'

Why had he said he would do this? He should never have agreed. Mum and Dad should never have encouraged him!

Why had they needed to tell him he was adopted? He had been eight at the time, old enough to understand, they said. His birth mummy had loved him, but it was impossible for her to keep him.

Recently, he found out the reason why. Social Services

had contacted Mum. Michael's biological mother wanted to meet him. Could they come in to talk about it?

Her name was Janet Henderson. She lived in Manchester. She was single, didn't have other children. She worked at B&Q. Did Michael have any questions? He'd wanted to say: Just the obvious one! What about my father? Why does no one mention him?

'What age is she?'

The social worker had looked in her file. 'Thirty.'

It took a moment to sink in. He was seventeen; she was thirty . . . thirteen; she was *thirteen* when she had him. He'd thought he was going to throw up.

'Will I drive you into town, drop you off?' Mum asked him now.

'No, I'll get the bus.'

She put her hand on his arm. He didn't look at her. She walked away, leaving him standing at the window as rain started to fall, pattering on the glass.

Janet had a good view of the street below from the guest house. People were closing umbrellas, going into shops, opening them again when they came out. She would walk down the pavement, around the corner to the Social Services building.

To meet her son.

Teenagers were coming out of a music shop. That could be him – picking one whose hair was a similar colour to her own. The next thought went through her mind before she could stop it – or did he take after his father?

What would she say if Michael asked about his father?

Janet had been warned by the social worker there might be questions she didn't feel comfortable answering. What would she say about him? Janet had asked herself this over and over.

She could repeat what she had said at the time. 'Someone at school.'

Her parents had pressed her. She had named half a dozen boys. Could be any of them. They wouldn't look at her after; didn't see her baby before he was taken away.

She couldn't lie to her son, though. How could she begin their relationship with a lie? She would tell him the truth. He would believe her. No one else would ever have believed her.

'I'll tell him the truth.' Janet said the words out loud. She could hear her heartbeat; was hot; light-headed. Wiped her clammy hands on a tissue. She needed to put on her coat and scarf. Needed to leave. Would he be there already when she arrived?

She looked down at the street below again, at the strangers going about their day. Her son could be one of them and she wouldn't recognise him. She had thought they'd send photographs. Had been too young to understand what adoption meant, to realise he would become someone else's baby – theirs completely. No one told her she'd never hear about him, or see him. She'd never have let him go if she'd known!

Her heart was pounding; she knew if she looked in a mirror her face would be drained of colour, tears evident behind her eyes. Had to pull herself together. Couldn't meet her son in this state. Her fingers worried the material of her skirt. She clasped her hands tightly together, rested her forehead against the windowpane. Its coldness soothed her, and the soft patter of rain against the glass.

Michael got off the bus, sheltering from the rain under a shop canopy, checked his watch. It was a short walk to the Social Services building. He would wait until the rain eased. Didn't want to be early.

What would she look like?

After he found out he was adopted, he saw a film about a woman with motor neurone disease whose husband had died. She had to give up her baby because she was so ill, had no choice. Michael understood then; this was what had happened to him. She had no choice. In his dreams he could see his mother's face, so like the woman's in the film, weeping for her baby.

A pulse beat in his temple. He knew differently now he'd found out her age, knew they'd been right at school. They had kept asking what his mother was called. 'He doesn't know,' they laughed when Michael didn't respond. 'We know, don't we. Slapper, that's her name. Or is it Slut? Which is it, Mike? You must know! She's *your* mother!'

His head began to throb. He welcomed the pain. It matched his anger. He would ask her straightaway, 'What's my father called?' Any of these men walking along the street could be him. Could be that guy over there with the beard, or him with his wife, putting up an umbrella.

Rain drummed louder on the shop canopy above his head.

A sudden deluge; water running down the pavement. Michael checked the time again. It'll be over soon, he told himself, repeating it out loud to hear his own voice, to try to still his racing mind. 'It'll be over soon.'

'Do you think so?' A woman's voice beside him.

She took down her coat hood, moving further back to escape the water pouring from the canopy overhead. Her coat was red, a blue scarf with red flowers around her neck. She glanced at her watch, talking to herself, sounding nervous. 'Too early . . .'

Shoulder-length hair, same colour as his. Tall, almost his height.

She fidgeted with the collar of her coat, with its belt, couldn't seem to still her hands. She clasped them together, took a deep breath. Noticed him staring. 'You've got caught out too,' she said.

Michael nodded, unable to speak. There was something about her . . . He studied her profile, as she watched the traffic going past, looked for similarities to his own. A prominent chin – same as him!

'Have you far to go?' Michael finally found his voice.

She shook her head. 'No, not far.'

He never thought it would be like this, that he'd feel an instant connection with her. She was obviously as nervous as him, her face pale, her hands couldn't keep at peace, were fidgeting again, with her coat cuffs, her scarf.

'The rain's easing. I'd better make a run for it.'

Michael's heart skipped a beat. *You're already there.* Opened his mouth to say it.

'Job interviews are hateful. Wish me luck!'

'Your father is dead.'

What Janet would tell Michael.

The truth.

It was raining harder, coming down in sheets. The guest

house window had misted. She rubbed it with her sleeve. A tall woman in a bright coat on the pavement below, rushing for cover under a shop canopy. She took down her hood, spoke to the boy who was already sheltering from the weather. Both had dark wavy hair.

What colour was his hair? Was he small or tall? The social worker had said Michael might ask questions like these about his father.

What if he asked if she'd loved his father?

Janet would tell the truth.

Everybody loved him. He was great fun, made everyone laugh. She had loved him; how could she not? She was Uncle Eddie's favourite girl.

He worked night shifts, picked her up from school in the afternoons when Mum and Dad were at work. They played games at his house – secret games. Dressing-up was his favourite. They'd open the special chest, and he'd choose a satin dress and glittery shoes with heels she couldn't walk in. He would help her take off her school uniform, sit her on his knee, telling her she was a bobby-dazzler, making her giggle at the funny words she didn't understand. 'Uncle Eddie wants to dress up too,' unbuttoning his shirt.

The rain had eased.

Janet checked her watch.

The woman in the red coat who had been sheltering under the shop canopy hurried from below it. The boy she had been talking to followed, standing on the pavement, as though in a daze. Stared after her, seeming oblivious to the other people hurrying past.

Janet needed to leave now, or she would be late. Stand, she told herself. Said it out loud. 'Stand up.'

She had held back tears to now. One leaked out . . . another . . . the people on the pavement below blurring, as she tried to picture herself walking to the corner of the street and out of sight, going to meet her son.

Michael and the social worker waited in the room he had been in before, in which he had found out his biological mother had been thirteen when she had him. They talked about Michael's school, the university he wanted to go to . . .

He sneaked a glance at the clock on the wall. Twenty minutes past the arranged meeting time.

The social worker had run out of things to say. She looked at the clock as well, fidgeted, excused herself.

Alone in the room, Michael's lips moved into a contemptuous smile. She wasn't going to show up. Made it justifiable to hate her. She couldn't even do the right thing now, seventeen years later.

He stood, walked to the door, along the corridor to reception.

Through the glass frontage of the Social Services building, people walked past on the pavement.

He quickened his pace. Another few steps and he would be outside.

'I . . . I'm Janet Henderson.'

Michael turned his head towards the voice. A small, fair-haired woman in a black coat was speaking to the receptionist.

'I- I'm here to . . .' She put a hand on the reception desk, as if to steady herself.

Michael walked on, opened the main door, stepped outside.

Took a deep intake of fresh air.

He glanced through the glass wall of the building as he made his way along the pavement. She was hunched over on a chair in the waiting area, her hands clenched together on her lap, gazing downwards. Even from this distance, he could see the tremble of her shoulders.

He walked quickly along the pavement.

There was a bus on the hour, every hour.

It pulled up at the stop.

He got on.

Sat down.

He had kept the appointment. He owed her nothing!

Forget about it. It's *over.*

What was he going to tell . . .

Mum had said to him this morning before he left home, 'I know how difficult this is.'

She would understand; he'd kept the appointment, had been there at the designated time.

'I'm so proud of you, Michael.'

More people got on.

The driver would close the doors.

He found himself standing, walking to the front of the bus.

He went back into the Social Services building, sat a couple of chairs away from her, gazed straight ahead.

'I'm Michael,' he heard himself say.

Her head turned towards him. He could feel her eyes on him.

'Th- thank you . . . for . . . for agreeing . . .' she eventually said, her voice barely audible.

He breathed in, breathed out, steadied himself, made himself turn towards her.

To look properly, for the first time, at his mother.

No One Will Know

MY CRIME IS I'm an overthinker.

Hardly a crime, you say. A character flaw, or an unfortunate personality trait. 'Crime' is the word going round in my overactive brain, the word no one else is using about what has happened.

Accident, is what they are saying, such a terrible accident.

I have always been like this, a worrywart, as my mother called me. She got child psychology books from the library. 'Clear your mind, Terry, imagine a blank canvas on which to project positive thoughts.' Each night, we did relaxation techniques, breathing exercises. 'Go out and play with your friends,' said my father.' (What friends?) 'Have some fun.' What he really meant was, try to be more like Ashley.

Even with all his groupies (I'm not exaggerating, his mates hung on my brother's every word, visibly relished any tiny part they got to play in his mad schemes and dare-devils)

Ash preferred my company. God knows why; I was a drag, even bored myself.

'Lighten up, bro,' when I frowned at his next big idea.

We did the usual rebel teen things, getting into scrapes, playing practical jokes on the neighbours – by *we*, I mean Ash, of course; I was just holding onto his coat-tails. I couldn't resist Ash, but then no one could, and I revelled in his love, really there was no other word for it, his brotherly love. 'Terry's coming out of his shell.' Relief in Mum's voice.

The schemes Ash liked best were the ones no one knew we were involved in, must be what serial killers felt like, no guilt, just didn't want to get caught.

Serial killers? you say. I know it is a ridiculous comparison, but the thinking behind our teenage pranks and the crimes of Jack the Ripper were the same.

No one will know.

All that mattered.

We had a family restaurant (home cooking, Dad was the chef, Mum served). We were virtually reared in it, just a few staff, like Quincy, who'd been there all our lives. Ash liked pranks involving food, but Quincy had his eagle eye on us. We'd pulled one trick too many, switching sugar for salt, docken leaves in the salad mix. Was in the restaurant, Ash heard someone talking about edible flowers. He cut up pansies, put them into the soup, we'd got the job of blending it. 'What if not all flowers are edible?' I'd tried my best to talk him out of it. 'Lighten up, bro.' I couldn't sleep that night. Our parents had eaten some of the soup. Crept into their room, kept watch, stood over them.

Ash snoring next door. I kept watch all night, the sound of my heartbeat in my ears.

Dad took a back seat in the business, because of his rheumatoid arthritis, had to spend an increasing amount of time in bed, Mum looking after him. We weren't old enough to shoulder the responsibility, but Ash stepped up, 'Tel and me'll take over,' relief on Dad's face. Ash was always going to take over one day anyway, a born chef, a natural with food, 'chip off the old block,' Dad liked to say, but he was a way better chef than Dad. I was 'front of house' Ash told people, like it was a posh restaurant, instead of glorified pub grub.

I was in the kitchen one morning, wiping clean the Specials board, when Ash arrived for work. I still lived at home. He had a flat, had shared with his girlfriend, when they split up he'd kept it on. He was carrying something.

'Where'd you get that?' He had taken off the outer bag. Inside was a large parcel of minced meat. Our beef supplier usually delivered.

'Got us a great deal,' he said. 'Where from?' I asked. 'Will save us loads,' said Ash. 'If we mix it with the quality stuff.'

Our burgers, lasagne, and chilli were made from prime beef, locally sourced, as highlighted on the menu. I pointed this out. 'Can't afford it,' said Ash. 'We'll mix it half and half. No one will know.'

'You can't do that! Prime beef, that's what it says on the–'

'Lighten up, bro. We're only talking about a few horse burgers.'

I was speechless.

'The face on you, Tel. I'm joking! You know I'm joking. It's low-grade, cheaper beef, that's all.'

'Why are you not using our supplier?'

'They only do the top-end stuff.'

'It's not right, Ash.'

'Look, we got through Covid, remember how hard that was? Closed for yonks, then only allowed half the covers, spacing them out. Now, the electric's through the roof; our suppliers have almost doubled their prices. If we don't cut costs we ain't gonna survive. This place will have to be sold, everything Mum and Dad built up. That what you want, Terry?'

'Course not! It's just–'

'No one will know,' he said again.

I should have taken the high moral ground, should have said *I* will know, or *we* will know, but there wouldn't have been any point. He didn't care.

They will know, the customers, I thought. Will taste the difference and complain. I tried to put a spoonful of lasagne into my mouth. When I first became vegetarian, Ash had said, 'We're head of the food chain, like it or not, just the way it is, bro.'

No complaints from the customers.

A new bag of meat on the bench. No wording, just a barcode on the label. I compared it with the good mince, prodded with a fork. Different texture; different colour. Ash behind me, whinnying, bent double laughing. That was the thing about Ash, everything was a joke. There had been a scandal the year before Covid, horse meat in ready meals in the supermarket. You were overreacting, you say.

I was. Knew I was. Of course, it wasn't horse meat.

Regulars, a couple, not in as usual, someone at the bar counter talking about them. 'The wife's not well. Bad stomach.' I almost dropped the tray of glasses in my hands. The last time they were in. The special. Janine had the special, the lasagne! We'd be exposed. Would be in all the papers!

Ash told me to calm down. 'She's got the runs, that's all. Anyway, you don't know she got it from here.'

'They'll test the food! They'll close us down!' Ash put his hands on my shoulders, 'Breathe in, Tel . . . slower . . . and out. She's got an icky gut, that's all. Will be in again in a few days, right as rain. I've been eating the burgers for weeks.' He patted his stomach. 'Fit as a fiddle.'

'But, Ash–'

'Lighten up, bro.'

All very well, him saying he had no ill effects, had a stomach of cast iron. Only thing he couldn't eat was mushrooms, had made him sick when he was a kid, hadn't touched them since.

A week later, still no sign of Janine coming through the door. 'Heard she's in hospital,' gossip at the bar.

Went into the kitchen, my stomach clenching, heart thumping. Ash, eating a bowl of chilli, a spoon in one hand, his mobile in the other. 'Can't hear you, you're breaking up, hold on.' He stood, went out into the back yard. I followed, 'Ash, I need to speak to you, now!' He waved me away.

His bowl of chilli on the table. I couldn't bear the smell, the sight of it. Dirty dishes, waiting to be scraped beside the sink, the fries from earlier. Ash's laughing voice carried through the open door, 'Yeah, they don't know the difference, the old gee-gees aren't a bad flavour.'

Mushrooms left on a plate.

Belly laughter from outside.

I cut the mushrooms into tiny pieces, dropped them into his bowl, gave it a good stir. Let's see how he liked having 'an icky gut'.

The next day, I got the bag of meat from the fridge, put it in the food waste. I didn't care what Ash said. I'd tell Dad if he got more of it; he would put an end to it.

I carried the Specials board outside.

Janine?

Janine walking up the pavement.

My face broke into a smile.

She looked thinner; put a hand on my arm. 'Oh Terry love, I've had a time of it. M'sister gave me chicken not cooked through. She were worse than me, she's still . . .'

In the kitchen, Quincy was rummaging in the fridge. 'Where's the meat?'

'We're not using it anymore.'

He laughed.

'What?'

'He got you.'

'Ash,' he continued. 'On the phone to me yesterday, knew you could overhear.'

Quincy gave my shoulder a playful push. 'I got him the contact for it, for the beef, a mate of mine is a butcher. Where is Ash anyway? It'll be opening time soon.'

I rang him.

No answer.

Went round to his flat; he'd be pale, groaning, and clutching his stomach. That's what you get for eating horse burgers, I'd say, play him at his own game. I laughed, rang his bell again . . .

Knocked the door.

He must be sleeping it off.

I went back to the restaurant, told Quincy we'd have to manage without him.

Rang Ash again, once the lunch rush was over. Still no reply. Mum had a spare key for his flat, I'd better go and check on him. Would have to own up about the mushrooms. It was the only practical joke I had ever solely played, and I'd played it on the king of practical jokers.

But we never got to have that conversation.

Mum used to encourage me to do this, to tell my worries, my feelings of anxiety to an imaginary person, the things you can't tell anyone else. It helped in the past, but I can't imagine anything will change how I feel, and do I really want to alleviate the guilt? It is what I deserve for my crime. Eaten something with mushrooms in it by mistake. A tragic accident, everyone is saying.

Ash had severe diarrhoea, evidence of it in his flat. Had taken a bath afterwards, during which he'd had another violent episode, causing him to pass out. What the coroner said had most likely happened.

No one knows it was my fault. I stay in my room. The

turning, churning of my thoughts have taken on a sound of their own, like an engine, an endless thrum.

I could confess, but it won't change anything, won't bring the dead to life, most likely wouldn't make me feel any better. Any less guilty. I know everyone will find out what I did. I know they will. Mum and Dad. Everyone, Ash.

It is not an imaginary person I'm telling this to.

It is Ash.

Lighten up bro, you say.

No one will know.

Miss Win

'I LOOK MISS ELSA.'

Win tutted to herself; Elsa hadn't told her they had a booking. The cottages were in order, ready for the start of the season, but they needed aired before new arrivals, the beds made up.

'I look Miss Elsa,' he repeated. El-*sa,* emphasis on the second syllable.

He had a rucksack, slung over one shoulder. Win had thought it was Elsa back when she'd heard a vehicle, but it had been a taxi. He was shorter than Win, like most men, unruly brown hair, dark eyes, swarthy skin. A foreigner. '*You can't say that nowadays, Win,*' Elsa's voice in her ear.

He opened his mouth, no doubt to say the same again. Win got in first. 'You have a booking with us?'

His brow wrinkled.

Win repeated, slower and louder.

His frown deepened.

Elsa took bookings on her computer, perhaps it translated for you, into different languages. She wouldn't put it past it, no one seemed able to exist nowadays unless they were *online*. Win had taken early retirement when the post office became computerised.

'What is your name?'

She pointed to herself. 'Win.'

He put his head to the side, like the spaniel she'd once had. She shouldn't compare him to a dog, that wouldn't be socially correct either.

He suddenly smiled, understanding. 'Miss Win,' saying it again, as if he liked the sound on his tongue, 'Miss Win.' If he had a tail, he'd wag it. 'Miss Win– '

'Enough!'

His face fell.

She pointed to him.

He was called Darren.

She hadn't the energy to extract a surname, gestured to the row of cottages along the lane.

He followed closely behind.

The keys – she hadn't brought them; explained this, but was wasting her time. He clearly didn't understand a word, began following her back towards the house. 'Stay,' she said firmly, put up her hand in a stop sign.

She glanced back. He was looking in a cottage window, hands cupped around his face.

He wasn't there when she returned. Win looked up the lane, towards the road leading to the village.

A tap on her shoulder.

Jeepers creepers!

Smiling, standing in a cottage doorway, beckoning to her to come in, as if *he* owned it and *she* were the visitor. Win tutted to herself, scatterbrain Elsa must have left Bluebell's door unlocked (Elsa had insisted on naming each cottage after a flower). Win walked along the row of five, checking the doors. The others were locked. He must have tried each door.

'What do you think you're doing?' she said.

Win followed him into the cottage.

He disappeared into the kitchen.

'*Darren?* You can't just . . .'

He brought something out of his rucksack. A mobile phone, pointed at it, then at the thingamajig on the shelf. 'Of course, we have to provide wi-fi, Win!' Elsa had said. 'They'll want a break from it, when they're on holiday,' Win replied. Elsa had looked at her as if she were an imbecile.

Darren was agitated, tugging at her cardigan sleeve, gesturing at his phone as if his life depended on having an internet connection. *Make allowances*, Win told herself. *A foreigner.* What was wrong with thinking or saying that anyway, he was from a foreign country after all. 'He's a *visitor*, Win,' Elsa's voice in her ear again. 'At least *try* to be civil.'

She opened the guest file, found the page with the code. His fingers scurried at his phone.

Win had a mobile. For emergencies. A birthday present from Elsa. Win made calls, could manage a text. *Suitable for the elderly*, it had said on the box; chunky buttons, easy to use. 'I am only sixty-four, Elsa,' she had felt like pointing out, 'just a few years older than yourself.' Elsa's mobile was like Darren's, slim and sleek. The opposite of Elsa in appearance.

Win showed Darren how to work the gas fire, explained about the immersion heater. Whether he understood or not was another matter.

He followed her around like a puppy; at one point she stopped to straighten a picture on the wall, he was so close behind he almost bumped into her.

Elsa had made up the beds, left a welcome tray in the kitchen, put milk in the fridge. She would have taken a deposit online. Win should really get him to sign the visitors' book, fill in his home address, but Elsa could sort that out when she returned from the village.

'It has been nice to meet you, Darren.'

He looked blank.

She held out her hand.

His face broke into a smile. He pumped her hand.

She tried to extricate hers.

'Enough!'

He let go, his expression falling.

She opened the cottage door, took a few paces outside.

He was behind.

'Stay.' She pointed at the cottage. Flopsy, her spaniel had been called, big brown eyes, intent on hers, waiting for a pet on the head when he obeyed a command.

Darren blinked; Flopsy's long eyelashes; he turned, went back into the cottage, closed the door.

Good boy.

Win peeled potatoes for dinner.

The kitchen window faced the yard.

Ah, there was Elsa now, pulling up in her car.

She came through the door. 'The guest arrived,' said Win.

'*Already?*' Elsa turned on her heel.

Typical; rushing to welcome Darren. Elsa went over the

top with all their guests, chatted over coffee at the cottage tables, got to know them. 'A warm welcome, first rule of hospitality, Win,' as though she were a business expert.

Win set the table.

Peeled carrots and parsnips.

Ah, Elsa outside again, closing Bluebell's cottage door behind her. Made her way along the lane towards the house. Flicked her hair over her shoulders, something she did a hundred times a day.

'Darren settled in?' asked Win, when Elsa came into the kitchen.

'You mean Dorin.'

'That's what I said.'

'His name is Dorin. *Dor-in.* At least have the courtesy to get it right.'

She was so touchy. Nothing Win said was ever right, offence could always be taken.

'How would *you* like to be called the wrong name?' Elsa went on, two spots of colour appearing on her heavily made-up cheeks, and Win felt her own face grow hot, glanced towards the dresser drawer, in which was her old badge, Postmistress Miss Winifred Munroe. *Marilyn*, the schoolboys used to call her, in the village shop, sniggering behind her in the queue. Wolf-whistled after her down the street, a standing joke, how opposite she was to the movie star, her height, mannish figure, oversized hands and feet, waistless body.

'How long is *Dor-in* staying?' Win asked.

'As long as he wants.'

'What do you mean?' They didn't take open-ended bookings.

'I won't be here for dinner,' said Elsa, glancing at the carrot in Win's hand.

Win waited for her to elaborate, but Elsa had turned, walking away . . . The creak of the stair treads.

When she came back down, Win waited for her to say who she was having dinner with. She had put a lot of effort into her appearance, was wearing a short pink dress, which was too young for her; all her clothes were age inappropriate. Large hoop earrings, multiple necklaces and bracelets; her dinner companion would need a gas mask to cope with the overwhelming perfume.

Win had been expecting this, had known it would only be a matter of time until Elsa had a new man. You'd think three failed marriages would be enough for anyone, especially after how devastated she was at the end of the last one. She hadn't seen it coming, her husband telling her they were incompatible. Win knew anyone else would have seen warning signs, but not Elsa, with her head in the clouds. She had arrived, distraught, on Win's doorstep, asked if she could stay a few days. That was six years ago. Cousin Elsa, how she had introduced herself in the village.

She got into her car; drove away.

Win put the potatoes on to boil, picked up the visitors' book on the dresser, wondered where their guest was from: Poland, Romania, Ukraine? A Polish girl had worked for a while in the village shop.

Elsa never bothered asking guests to write their details in the book, even after Win had reminded her how important it was to have the home address and telephone number of a relative in case of emergency. Elsa had sighed, calling her a fusspot. Win had felt like replying, 'Better than being a scatterbrain.'

Win put the visitors' book under her arm, went outside.

The plaques on the cottage doors had been hand-painted by Elsa. Win cringed each time she heard her say to new guests, 'You're in Daffodil,' or, 'This is the key for Tulip.'

The flowers weren't well-painted; the bunch of what were meant to be bluebells looked like something a child had done. It had been Elsa's idea to renovate Win's row of derelict cottages, convert them into holiday homes, had used her divorce money to fix them up. They split what the cottages brought in.

She knocked.

As she waited for him to answer the door, Win thought of Elsa, driving her car, flicking back her hair; who was she on the way to meet? Must be in town, where there were several restaurants; the village pub didn't serve food.

Win knew the villagers must talk about Elsa, a sixty-year-old woman who often sported a ponytail. (Sometimes, Win could barely refrain from grabbing the scissors and chopping it off.) They would laugh behind their hands at the too-young clothes, too-low tops, her sagging, creased cleavage on full view; the garishly painted nails, lately each finger was a different colour. 'It's the fashion,' had been the reply when Win commented. 'Amongst teenagers, I presume?' Win had felt like retorting. Her husband had left her for someone older. Elsa hadn't been able to take this in, but Win understood; her spare room now had pink frilly curtains and bedspread, a dream catcher suspended from the ceiling. Elsa even had a teddy. Win really didn't blame him.

The cottage door opened.

'Hello Dar-, Dorin.'

Win brought the book from under her arm. 'Would you mind?' She showed him the names and addresses inside.

He looked puzzled.

She realised she'd forgotten to bring a pen with her.

'May I come in?' she indicated into the cottage. There was a pen and comments sheet in each cottage.

He stood aside to let her through, followed her into the kitchen. She got the pen, opened the book on the table.

He gazed at the page.

Win thought of her potatoes on the cooker.

She took back the pen. NAME: '*Dorin?*'

He shook his head.

'You don't want to tell me your surname?' Or maybe he didn't understand. *Make allowances, Win.*

'Where are you from? Poland?'

'I come Romania.'

She wrote it down.

NEXT OF KIN: 'What is your father's name?'

He frowned.

'Mother . . . Mum?'

'Mămică!' he cried, put his hand into his pocket, brought out his phone, his fingers hurrying at it in that annoying way everyone did.

He held it too close to Win's face, whatever he was trying to show her was a blur. She pushed his hand further away. A photograph on the screen, of a woman in a headscarf and old clothes. *Poor,* the first thought to jump into Win's head. *She looks a bit like me,* the second. Large, mannish, stray wisps of faded blonde hair escaping from the scarf. Win's hair used to be her crowning glory, long and luscious, until she started getting the Marilyn taunts, had cut it off.

'Mămică!' He pointed, excited, like a child.

Win needed to check her potatoes weren't boiling dry.

A sound from the direction of the cottage door. Dorin also turned his head.

'Meals on wheels!'

Elsa came into the room, carrying a brown paper bag reeking of fish and chips.

Win could only stare.

'I show Miss Win,' said Dorin, holding up his phone.

Elsa kept her back to Win, got glasses from a cupboard, cutlery from a drawer.

'A word please, Elsa. Outside.'

Win was made to wait.

'He's a friend,' said Elsa, sharply.

'Not a *paying* customer?'

'No.' Even sharper.

'Where did you meet him?'

Elsa looked away.

'In town?'

'It's none of your–'

'He's staying in *my* cottage.'

Dorin was at the open doorway of the cottage. Not that he'd be able to understand what they were saying. Anyway, he was busy with his phone.

A terrible thought occurred to Win.

She pointed to his mobile, then to Elsa.

It took a moment for him to get her meaning.

He smiled, nodded.

Of course. Win might have guessed.

She had met him *online*.

It was late by the time Elsa came into the house. Win was waiting. Elsa walked past, as though she was going to go upstairs to bed and not say anything, not explain anything.

'How long have you known him?'

Elsa ignored her, went to walk on.

'How long have you been giving him money?'

Win may not be on the internet, but it had been on the news, in the papers. Scammers. They bled you dry. People had lost their entire savings, even their houses! Win had seen a TV documentary. Lonely people, vulnerable people, taken in by criminals. Romance scams, they were called. Elsa was a sitting duck.

'How much–'

'You don't understand.'

'Tell me, Elsa. I *want* to understand. You have been giving him money, and now he's here. Why is he here?'

A defiant look Win knew only too well crossed Elsa's face.

'For us to be together.'

Win laughed. It burst from her, couldn't help herself. In the documentary there had been middle-aged, elderly even, men, who believed a nubile twenty-something had fallen in love with them. She knew Elsa was a flibbertigibbet, but had credited her with *some* common sense.

'He is *half* your age, Elsa. Take a look at yourself; take a good look in the mirror. You are *sixty*, Elsa.'

Elsa's face flushed, her eyes sparking.

'That may be, but at least I'm not a dried-up old spinster.'

Cut to the quick. The phrase jumped into Win's mind. Elsa turned on her heel, went upstairs.

She didn't mean it. They'd been happy before, she and Elsa . . . *happy* was too strong a word. *Contented.*

Tomorrow, he would have to go.

At breakfast, Elsa avoided Win's eye. Win had expected an apology, but Elsa's expression was still defiant.

'They may be *your* cottages, Win, but I paid to renovate them, to furnish them. If I wish to have a friend to stay, I don't think it is asking too much.'

'You are being scammed, Elsa!' Win wanted to reply, but knew she had to be careful what she said, otherwise Elsa would clam up, or flounce from the table; knew how stubborn her cousin was. If Win said out loud, 'He'll have to go,' it would make Elsa even more determined for him to stay. Win had discovered how unmoveable Elsa was during her divorce, procrastinating over every miniscule detail, made it as long-drawn-out and acrimonious as possible.

Win softened her voice. 'What do you know about this man, Elsa?'

'He is one of the most caring people I have ever met.' Her face broke into a smile. 'He looks after his family, his mother and cousins. They depend on him.'

Win tutted to herself at Elsa's naivety; in the documentary, this was how scammers took in their victims, an aunt or granny or whoever were sick, needed an emergency operation, they were too poor to pay.

'How much money have you given him?' Win had to

press her lips tightly together, not let the question escape, instead asked in a just-for-interest's-sake tone of voice, 'How long have you known him?'

'A year.'

Win tried to keep her face from showing shock.

Elsa had kept this from her all that time.

Win got into her car, drove towards town.

A bright March day; gorse flaring, the sea glinting in the distance. The time of year Win liked best, before the tourists arrived, clogging the roads, abandoning their vehicles to take photographs of the view. But today she couldn't appreciate the scenery. 'Herbie will know what to do,' she said out loud.

At breakfast time, Elsa had put eggs and bacon into a basket, walked with a spring in her step along the lane, to the cottage door.

Win had to wait to see Herbie. After Elsa had disappeared inside the cottage, she had gone up to her cousin's room.

An even bigger mess than usual, clothes strewn over the chair and bed, pots and tubes of creams and make-up crammed on the dressing-table. *Rejuvenates mature skin*, it said on one. Win had shaken her head, will take more than that to make you look half your age, Elsa. Win searched the chest of drawers, made sure she put everything back the exact same way she had found it. Opened the wardrobe, searched the handbags piled inside. Where else . . . She suddenly realised: Elsa would get her bank statements *online*. They had wanted to do this with Win, stop sending them by post.

'Win?'

'Ah, Herbie. At last.'

She followed him into his office.

He indicated the chair at the other side of his desk. A man of few words, just like he'd been a boy of few words. She had sat beside him on her first day at school.

'The thing is . . .' She explained about Elsa being scammed, and now the man in question was here, staying in Win's cottage.

'You have evidence she is being scammed?'

'Yes . . . well, no, not exactly, but I know that's what's happening.' Win's gaze moved to the plaque on his desk, Station Officer Herbert McKendry. 'I need you to arrest him, Herbie!'

He turned to a computer screen, pressed buttons on a keyboard. 'Name?'

'Dorin.'

He raised an eyebrow.

'I don't know his surname. It'll be fake anyway. You have to do something before he takes all of Elsa's money!'

Herbie's eyebrow stayed raised.

'He's from Romania!'

'*Racist*,' Elsa's voice in her ear.

'She's smitten by him, says he supports his family. He hasn't two beans to rub together, you know just to look at him. It will be Elsa who is supporting his imaginary family. You have to arrest him, Herbie!'

'I can only do that if a crime has been committed.'

'But–'

'What do you expect me to do, Win? Arrest him because Elsa likes him?'

Win got back into her car. She needed Elsa's bank statements, evidence that money was being transferred to a fraudster's account. Should have gone to the computer classes the post office wanted her to take.

Driving through the village; a couple strolling with their backs to her along the pavement. A woman in red trousers, too tight, too young for her.

Elsa and *him,* walking hand in hand.

Win gingerly pressed the button on the computer.

Yes, it lit up.

Jeepers creepers!

It was him, Dorin, his face on the screen!

She pressed the letter B on the keyboard. Nothing happened. She continued. A-N-K.

Still nothing.

Where was the off button? Elsa would know she had been tampering with it! Win pressed random buttons. The screen stayed lit up, *him* grinning at her.

Win thought of Elsa tripping along the pavement in her high heels, holding his hand, sashaying her wide hips, ponytail swinging. She'd be a laughing stock in the village; would make both her *and* Win a laughing stock.

'Were you on my computer, Win?'

'No, of course not. You know I can't . . .'

Accusation still in Elsa's eyes.

'I, er . . . think I pressed something, by accident, when I was cleaning.'

'You're a terrible liar, Win.'

'Dinner's almost ready, fishcakes, your favourite, Elsa. I thought we could have a good chat . . .'

'I'll not be here for dinner.'

She ate with him every night.

They went to the village for supplies. Win watched them leaving . . . arriving back, carrying bags of shopping into the cottage.

Win had expected to like the peace and quiet, there'd often been times she'd wished she could have a meal on her own, the way she used to before Elsa arrived, one hand propping a book, no Elsa rabbiting on, no Elsa leaving lipstick stains on the china, no Elsa flicking her hair, strands of which ended up everywhere, in the food, clogging the drains. But Win no longer enjoyed solitary meals, had got used to having Elsa around.

Win was alone during the day as well. Elsa used to make jewellery at the kitchen table, Win used to grumble about the mess. Now, Elsa got *him* to help her make necklaces, bracelets, earrings, from shells, glass, feathers even, that she collected on the beach. Hideous-looking pieces. People bought it online. The craft shop in the village sold it to tourists. No accounting for taste.

Now, it would be the cottage table covered in hooks, clasps, bits of wire, junk from the beach. They went for walks in the afternoons, Elsa behaving like a lovestruck teenager, making a fool of herself. Win cringed at the window, as they paused to kiss at the end of the lane. On the beach, Elsa would be barefoot on the sand. He would carry her sandals, pausing to kiss again, for everyone to see.

It was Easter next week; he would have to leave then, they

would need all the cottages for paying guests. Elsa wouldn't be able to argue with that.

Dorin would pay Win her share of the cottage rent, Elsa announced. Win opened her mouth to say, 'You mean *you* will.' 'From his earnings, making jewellery,' Elsa went on, clearly took great pleasure telling Win this, her face and voice smug. 'They are *my* cottages, I can ask him to leave if I want,' Win almost replied, but knew Elsa would remind her she had invested in them, it was a joint business.

Elsa stayed late each night in the cottage. At least she hadn't moved in with him. Win had to be grateful for that.

The holiday season started, and Elsa began working each afternoon in the village craft shop which sold her jewellery. Win knew she usually enjoyed this part-time job, but now Dorin was on the scene she wouldn't want to leave him, but nor could she let down the shop owner who had been very supportive of her 'creative talent', as Elsa called it.

'Dorin will help with the cottages.'

Win almost retorted, 'Indeed, he will not.' Then again, this would be her chance to find out what he was up to. Beds needed changed when guests left, floors swept and mopped, an arm's-length list of tasks. He was eager to please, to follow instruction, his spaniel act, as Win thought of it. It didn't wash with Win, knew beneath this veneer was a conniving fraudster.

She enquired about his family as they dusted. Win had already asked Elsa the same question, keeping suspicion from her voice, feigning mild interest. According to Elsa they were farmers, had fallen on hard times when their crop failed. His father was dead, his cousins worked the farm.

'Your family are farmers?'

He looked puzzled, pretended not to know what she meant.

'They keep animals? Cattle, sheep?'

'Ænimel.'

At last, she was getting somewhere, opened her mouth to ask, 'Crops?' He pointed at a broken cat ornament on a shelf. 'I fix ænimel?'

Keeping watch at the kitchen window.

Elsa had left for work. A short while later, Dorin emerged from the cottage, walked along the lane, onto the road, disappeared from sight. He could be meeting someone, an accomplice, plotting her and Elsa's demise for all Win knew!

She followed; would see where he went, who he talked to.

He went into the village pub.

Win tried to tell herself she could go in, order an orange juice, find out who he was meeting, but she had never been in a public house in her life.

Win was upstairs the next day, came down to find him in her home, searching a kitchen drawer.

'What do you think you're doing?'

He looked alarmed. Had been caught red-handed.

'There's no money. None, anywhere here!'

He pretended not to know what she was talking about, his face distressed, his hands making a ball shape, waving it in her face.

'I want you to leave.' She pointed at the door. 'Do you understand? Leave the cottage. Now!'

'Please, Miss Win. I stay. *Please* . . .'

'String,' Elsa said that night. 'He was looking for a ball of string, Win! To fix a blind.'

How could she be so gullible?

'Perhaps, it would be better if we left.'

We.

Win should let them go. Elsa wasn't her responsibility, was a grown woman, almost a pensioner for crying out loud! When he left her penniless, she would come crawling back to Win, weeping and wailing, same as when she'd arrived. If she wanted to ruin her life, it wasn't up to Win to save her.

Win opened her mouth to say, 'Yes, just go.' She had lived alone for over ten years after her parents passed away in the same month, until Elsa came to stay, would be fine on her own again.

What if Elsa didn't come back?

'String, of course . . . my mistake,' she heard herself say.

'You'll apologise to Dorin?'

He grasped both her hands before she could stop him. 'Thanking to you, Miss Win.'

Win arranged her face into a return smile; even Elsa fell for it, beaming, same as Dorin. Just you wait, she silently told him. I'm going to catch you out.

It didn't take long. The following week, he rolled up his sleeves to mop a cottage floor. A watch on his wrist. He didn't usually wear one. He fiddled with it, adjusting the strap.

'New?' Win asked. It looked an old watch. Her mouth

almost dropped open when she saw the maker's name on the face.

'Where did you get it, Dorin?'

He didn't know what she was talking about.

She pointed at the watch.

'Village,' he replied.

There was no jewellers or antique shop in the village where he could have bought this.

'You buy?'

She was doing it now, speaking in broken English.

He shook his head. 'Man give to I.'

She wasn't going to make the same mistake as last time, of openly accusing him.

'Herbie. It's Win.'

She explained that Dorin had stolen an expensive watch.

'Has he admitted it?'

'He said a man gave it to him in the village. Gave him a *Rolex,* Herbie!'

'I'll check if there have been any reported thefts or burglaries. Leave it with me, Win.'

Nothing back from Herbie all afternoon. Win was about to ring the station again, when a police car pulled up and the man himself got out. Relief! It would be over, Herbie would arrest him. Win and Elsa would go back to how they were before.

Herbie opened the back door of the car.

A woman emerged.

She and Dorin must be in on it together.

The woman said they were on a family holiday, staying

in the village. She had only let her father out of her sight for a minute and he disappeared. Lately, he'd been giving away everything he owned. When she finally found him he no longer had his coat, his hat, and most importantly, his watch.

The other car door opened; a frail-looking man began to get out. 'Dad, I told you to stay in the car.' Dorin gave back the watch, the old man trying to insist he keep it. The woman shook Dorin's hand, said they didn't blame him, her father could be very persuasive, no harm was done, they'd got the watch back.

As they drove away, Dorin turned to Win, his face distressed. 'I not steal.'

'He give you,' said Win, despite herself.

He didn't steal the watch, but he *was* taking Elsa's money under false pretences. Elsa was supporting his supposed family, would be transferring money into his bank account every month, every week even. Win would get the account details, where all Elsa's money was going, would prove he was a fake.

Win went out to the cottage. Elsa had left for work. Dorin was making earrings at the kitchen table, bending minute wires with tiny pliers. Good with his hands, Win had to give him that, but then he didn't have paddles like hers on his wrists.

She pointed to the finished necklaces on the table. 'Mama like?' His face lit up at the mention of his mother, brought out his mobile, showed her the same fake photo she saw the day he arrived. 'Miss Elsa help?' Win pointed at the photograph.

He nodded, beamed.

She indicated herself. 'I help.'

He jumped up from his chair, and before Win could stop him, put his arms around her.

'What do you think you're–!'

'Thanking to you, Miss Win.'

He was childlike in height, compared to her, his head barely reaching her shoulder. She was conscious as he hugged her that the side of his face was almost touching her chest. She didn't think of them as breasts. 'Two fried eggs,' someone had laughed when they were in the school showers. Win had never forgiven the insult; might have, if her breasts had continued to grow like everyone else's, but this was the way they had remained, she'd never needed a bra.

'Enough!' said Win.

He released her, a smile still wreathing his face.

'I need your surname and bank account details.'

His brow creased.

She pointed to herself. 'Win Munroe.' At him. '*Dorin . . . ?*'

He said something beginning with B.

On the cottage comments sheet she got him to write it down, Dorin Barbaneagra, and his bank account details.

She hurried over to the house, got on the phone to Herbie.

He rang her back the next day. 'It's all above board, Win.'

'But he is draining Elsa's savings!'

'Freely giving someone money isn't a crime, Win.'

'Is *anything* in your book a crime, Herbie?'

Elsa no longer came back to the house at night, had moved into the cottage with him. During the day, Win tried to keep occupied, doing housework; was kept busy with the cottage bookings, cleaning, washing bedclothes, but the evenings were very long. She had always been a reader, but couldn't concentrate on a book, couldn't find the solace there she used to. *Turn on the television*, she told herself, but didn't get up from her chair, the room dimming around her, the only sound the odd creak of the house.

After lunch one day she went upstairs, got into bed. She would have a lie down, just for ten minutes . . .

Each afternoon she found herself getting under the covers.

A sound downstairs.

She went out to the landing.

Dorin, below in the hallway. He'd be going through each room, trying to find money, assessing the worth of her ornaments; strangely, she didn't seem to care.

'Miss Win sick?'

Why would he think that? It was as if he knew she'd been in bed. She ran a hand through her hair, straightened her cardigan. 'I'm fine.' They had been cleaning Daffodil earlier for new guests arriving tomorrow. Now that she thought about it, he had kept glancing at her as they worked.

She waited for him to leave, but he kept looking expectantly up at her, as if for a command.

'Brush yard for me?'

He nodded eagerly.

She went back into her bedroom.

'The blues,' her mother called it, the first time, when she'd had to take time off work. 'Just the blues. They'll pass.' Pills from the doctor that had made her constipated, made her feel worse.

Each day, Win was determined to keep busy, to keep on her feet all day, but after lunch found herself going upstairs, such a relief to lie down, close her eyes.

She dreamt of her mother, sitting at Win's bedside the way she used to, telling her it wouldn't be long now, until she felt better, would be back to her old self. She held Win's hand; it was very comforting, the feel of her hand in hers.

'Miss Win?'

She opened her eyes.

'Miss Win sick?'

Her gaze moved to his hand holding hers on top of the duvet.

His fingers pressed.

A tear squeezed from her eye, trickled down her cheek.

It began to edge earlier in the day; she wanted to go back upstairs after breakfast. No one would notice anyway, except when the cottages needed attention. She barely saw Elsa. She was too busy with her jewellery making, her job, her new man. Win didn't let herself give in to the draw of the staircase, kept busy, somehow kept going each day until lunchtime.

The last time she'd had 'the blues', Flopsy used to lie on the end of the bed, gazing at her with his depthless eyes. It was the only thing that had got Win out of bed, having to feed him, take him for a walk, had to pull herself together for his sake, was alone in the house, there was no one else to look after her beloved dog.

She was dozing over when she heard someone on the stairs.

Dorin at the doorway.

'Tea for Miss Win.'

He set a tray on the bedside table, Win's tray. He'd made tea in her kitchen, but she couldn't bring herself to care, to feel cross. He waited for her to sit up, propped the pillows behind her.

Self-conscious, as he watched her sip from the cup.

He had put sandwiches on a plate. As if knowing she'd skipped lunch. She had to eat one because he'd gone to the trouble.

The next day he appeared again. On the tray was a flower, one of Win's dahlias in the small vase from the kitchen dresser. She had to blink rapidly. He had brought a box to show her, with shells stuck to it. Absolutely hideous. 'You make these to sell?' He nodded; beamed. 'Lovely,' said Win.

The following day she pretended she was asleep, didn't want it to become a daily occurrence . . . the rattle of the china on the tray being taken away again.

She woke; someone was . . .

Jeepers creepers!

He was lying on the bed beside her! She went to speak, 'What do you think you're–?!' He was asleep. She opened her mouth again; he couldn't just lie down beside her! But he looked so peaceful, she hadn't the heart to waken him. Stubble on the side of his face, his chin; her gaze moved to his throat, to the strange protuberance of his Adam's apple.

She closed her eyes, knew she wouldn't go back to sleep, but must have, because she woke again; his face was turned towards her on the pillow, watching her. He smiled. Had such a kind face. She mustn't cry.

It was almost the end of the season, the cottages weren't busy, soon there wouldn't be a reason for Win to get up in the morning, wouldn't have to drag herself around until lunchtime. In the afternoons she was used to wakening, seeing Dorin lying beside her. Win knew she reminded him of his mother, somehow wasn't offended that he thought her similar to the old crone in the photograph.

Shouting.

Jeepers creepers!

Win's eyes flew open.

Elsa.

Elsa, standing beside the bed, her face inflamed, as if she'd caught Win and Dorin – what was the phrase – *in flagrante.* Dorin was on top of the covers fully dressed, they were only holding hands, why was she making such a fuss? Screaming at Dorin, 'How could you?' Running down the stairs, Dorin following.

Win went over to the bedroom window. The muffled sound of Elsa shouting outside, cottage guests getting into their car, staring, as she told Dorin she never wanted to see him again, was getting no more money!

He followed her into the cottage. Win expected Dorin to appear again, to come over to the house, to stay the night in the spare room. She kept watch until it was dark, but neither he nor Elsa emerged from the cottage.

Win knew the guests in Tulip were leaving the next morning, that Elsa would see them before they went.

Ah, there she was now, coming out of the cottage, flicking back her hair, knocking on Tulip's door . . . going inside . . .

coming out again with the guests, waving as they drove away. Win waited for her to look in her direction, see her at the kitchen window.

Win went outside, called to Elsa, could she have a word . . . Explained nothing had happened, explained how she hadn't been feeling well lately and Dorin had been very kind, but Elsa was as angry as the day before. 'I've told him he's to be gone by tonight.' Win repeated that nothing had happened. Elsa replied, 'Of course it didn't,' a sardonic smile, as though no man could possibly be attracted to Win. 'But it wasn't for lack of trying on your part. How did you lure him into your bedroom, Win? Did you pay him, was that it?'

The shock of Elsa's words, the cruelty of them, was too much. Win turned away, went back into the house.

Lying on her bed that afternoon, Win thought she heard Dorin's tread on the stairs . . . just the creaking of the house. He was leaving tonight, Elsa had said. Win needed him; she scrunched the quilt in her hand, needed the comfort of his hand holding hers.

Tears flowed down her cheeks, damping the pillow. It kept replaying in her head – Elsa's cruel words, the contemptuous smile, her angry expression. Win closed her eyes. If only she could sleep . . . The hours dragged past. . . Win stared at the ceiling. Elsa's face appeared on it, wouldn't give her peace . . .

Downstairs, the house phone began to ring, startling Win. Rang on and on. She wiped her eyes, made herself get up, went down to the hall.

'*Win.*' She recognised the voice, Jessica, the dog walker from the village, sounding breathless, sounding frantic. 'Win, the most terrible . . . it . . . it's Elsa, she . . . I've rung for an ambulance.'

Win went outside, stood, gazing towards the road, towards the cliff down to the sea.

Bluebell cottage door opened.

Dorin came over.

Put his hand on her arm when he saw the tears on her cheeks.

'Elsa has . . . fallen off the cliff.' That was what Jessica had said. 'Oh Win, she must have fallen from the cliff!'

Win tried to read Dorin's expression, to gauge from his reaction if he loved Elsa, but he looked blank.

'She's dead,' said Win, maybe he didn't understand. 'Oh Win, I've called . . . but it's too late,' Jessica had said.

He turned his head towards the road, towards the cliff; the wail of an ambulance could be heard in the distance.

'They'll be here soon, the police,' she thought out loud.

'Not I, Miss Win!'

Last night, Elsa had shouted that she never wanted to see him again, he was getting no more money, and now she was dead at the foot of the cliff.

'Where were you today, Dorin?'

'I clean Tulip.'

There had been a police investigation when a tourist had fallen from the cliff a few years ago.

'I try please Miss Elsa. She say I must go.'

'Did you see anyone?' asked Win. Tulip's guests had left; the other cottages were unoccupied.

Dorin shook his head.

What if they thought he . . . 'All afternoon? You cleaned all afternoon?' What if they thought it was him, that he . . . pushed her over. Win had told Herbie he was draining Elsa's savings. Yesterday, guests heard Elsa yelling at him to leave.

'Miss Elsa go village. I clean Tulip.'

His head turned towards the road again, as if picturing Elsa going to work that day. The countless times Win had watched her make her way along the lane, countless times she had tutted to herself about Elsa's lack of suitable footwear. Slingbacks or flimsy sandals that laced around her ankle. She didn't own a flat pair of shoes.

Oh, Elsa, Win's knees gave way, held onto Dorin's shoulder for support; he put his arm around her, there were tears in his eyes as well, his face pale. Those stupid sandals, Win had always been on at her to buy a pair of walking shoes, had even said to her, 'One of these days you'll fall and break your neck!' Surely, the police wouldn't think anything other than she accidently fell . . . But Win had repeatedly tried to convinced Herbie that Dorin was up to no good. What if they thought he'd something to do with it? Win couldn't let him be blamed; he was the kindest person she had ever met.

'Elsa left for work, then Dorin and I spent all afternoon giving Tulip a thorough clean.'

Win couldn't quite believe she was telling this story to the police, but she had to, for Dorin's sake, had gone over and over with him the chores they did together, before the police arrived, stripping beds, dusting, hoovering, over and over, so their stories would match. '*You're a terrible liar, Win*,' Elsa's voice in her ear, but when Herbie asked was she sure

Dorin never left her sight, Win had looked Herbie steadfastly in the eye. 'Absolutely. We had just finished cleaning, when Jessica . . .'

Dorin moved into the house.

In the evenings, Win read, and Dorin was on his phone. Elsa's computer was in her bedroom; she should offer it to him to use. Win would have to face it one of these days, sorting through Elsa's belongings, was several months since . . .

Dorin's mother had sent thanks to Win for helping her family. Dorin had shown Win the message on his phone, was in Romanian of course. Dorin had translated, 'Miss Win most kind lady . . .'

Win steeled herself before opening Elsa's bedroom door. The room had been unaired, there was still a faint scent of Elsa, her bottle of Peach Paradise *Eau de Parfum* on the dressing-table amidst the chaos of pots and jars.

Win sat on the dressing-table stool, gazed at Elsa's toiletries, telling herself not to cry. Had done nothing but cry the first month after Elsa's accident. It was Dorin who had got her through, making her meals, insisting she eat, lying beside her on her bed, holding her hand, grieving together. At night, as she tossed and turned, Win had hoped Dorin would hear – left her bedroom door ajar – hoped he would come and comfort her, the same way he did during the day, could see the spare room door across the landing.

Win's reflection in the mirror.

Turned her face one way, then the other.

A pot of cream on the dressing-table – *smooths fine lines and wrinkles* – Win spread it over her cheeks. Twisted up a lipstick. Dabbed perfume behind each ear. Lifted the lid of a large box. Elsa's jewellery, jumbled together.

A necklace of shells. Clip-on earrings to match.

If Dorin noticed anything different about her as they ate dinner, he didn't show it.

'Please, would you pass salt.'

'*The* salt,' said Win. She was teaching him English. It was a slow process, was a very difficult language to learn.

The earrings were nipping her lobes.

'Please, would you pass the salt, Miss Win?'

Beamed, pleased with himself.

That evening, she called for him from her bedroom.

Called louder. 'Dorin!'

'What wrong?'

'What *is* wrong?' she automatically corrected. 'I feel sad, Dorin.'

She patted the bed.

He lay down beside her.

She reached for his hand, brought it over to her side of the bed, clasped it on top of the duvet.

After a while, brought it under the covers, held it against her chest, her heart thumping; he'd be able to hear it, feel it, but his eyes stayed closed . . . His breathing altered, he was asleep.

The following night, she called for him again. This time her nightie was open under the covers; she held his hand against her nakedness . . . brushed his finger over her nipple, light, feathery strokes. Her breath caught in her throat.

He took his hand away.

She brought it back.

The weight of his body on top of hers, pressing . . . her legs opening, her hands tightening on his shoulders. Oh, oh, the intense scent of peaches, the friction of shells against her throat. Oh, oh . . .

Always on his phone.

Fingers flying over the screen, or talking on it. Seemed like a different person when he spoke his own language, rapid-fire sentences, looked, sounded confident, assured; older. He glanced behind, his expression changing when he saw her.

Furtive, thought Win.

He went outside.

Win at the window; his mouth opening, closing; she tried to lip read, not that she'd be able to understand.

Each night she waited for him . . . called for him . . . went across the landing when he didn't appear.

Always asleep. Or pretending to be.

He ended the call when he saw her approach.

'Are you hiding something from me, Dorin?'

He didn't understand.

She pointed at his phone.

The look on his face. Apprehension. Guilt.

It all came out.

The shock of his words almost made Win cry out, as if in pain. She had tried to tell Elsa how gullible *she* was, being fooled by him.

Win struggled to take in what he was saying.

He was going home. Had wanted to tell Win, but didn't

want to hurt her feelings. He missed his family. Miss Win most kind, he appreciated everything she had done for him.

Win should have known, should have guessed this would happen.

'I miss Mămică.'

'I'm glad you've been honest with me.' Win collected herself. 'Honesty is very important, I'm sure your mother taught you that. The thing is Dorin, I've been feeling bad about not being honest with the police. The day Miss Elsa . . .'

His face changed, grew worried.

'Remember, how we told the police you were with me. I shouldn't have lied. We need to tell the truth, that you weren't with me that day.' She didn't like having to say this, to see his little face crumble.

'I not hurt Miss Elsa!'

'I believe you, you know I do.' Win gave a sympathetic smile. 'But it doesn't look good, I'm afraid. You were overheard arguing, cottage guests heard Elsa telling you to leave.'

Dorin's face became more stricken. 'Last time I see Miss Elsa, she leave cottage, she go village.'

He looked along the lane, as though picturing Elsa.

Win followed his gaze.

Win had watched Elsa going to work that day, disappearing from sight at the end of the lane. Couldn't believe Elsa hadn't come to apologise for her cruel words, for the hideous things she had said earlier, couldn't bear there was such bad feeling between them.

Win had followed, along the road . . . onto the cliff path, quickening her pace when she caught sight of her cousin up ahead, hunkered down, fiddling with the sandal lace around her ankle.

'*Elsa . . . ?*'

Win reached her.

'Elsa, please, I can't cope with this. I- I've been feeling down lately . . . so very low. Please, let us be friends.'

'How much did you pay him?'

Win gasped; was like being slapped.

'How much did you pay to get him into your bed?' Elsa's face was contorted with anger. Win had seen her eyes sparking fury like this before, over her husband's new wife.

'How much, *Marilyn*?'

She must have heard this in the village. Win's skin prickled with humiliation, what the schoolboys had called her, everyone must call her that even now, behind her back, laugh about her. Win moved closer to Elsa, her arm rising, to strike Elsa, to slap her, to hurt her in return.

Shock registered on Elsa's face, her eyes on Win's raised hand, stepping quickly back; at the same time, Win thought, *I'm not really going to slap her, am I?* Elsa took another step back, was close to the edge, 'Elsa, come away from–' Elsa's foot twisting in her sandal, her body tilting, Win rushed forward, to grab hold of her, but she was falling backwards . . .

She disappeared over the side of the cliff.

Elsa lay on the rocks below.

There was no way down from here. *Ambulance*, Win couldn't breathe. *Ring for an ambulance*, searched her pockets, *need to ring for–* didn't have her mobile with her– *need to . . .* Elsa face up, eyes unmoving, blood pooling around her head.

Win ran back to the house, went to pick up the phone; she would have to say she was with Elsa, they'd been arguing, that she'd stepped back because Win was going to slap her. She couldn't tell them that, what would she tell them? Elsa's eyes unmoving . . . *She's dead. Too late for an ambulance.* Retracted her hand, found herself going upstairs, getting into bed.

'I not hurt Miss Elsa,' Dorin repeated now.

It would be forever imprinted on Win's mind, Elsa disappearing over the cliff, Elsa lying on the rocks, the broken-doll twist of her neck. If she had been wearing sensible shoes it would never have happened, but she would never listen to Win.

She couldn't lose Dorin as well.

'If you go away, Dorin, I'll have no one to talk to. I might find myself at the station, talking to the police. We shouldn't have lied, said I was with you that day. They can visit us, I'll pay for your mother and cousins to come for a visit. How about that?'

He shook his head.

She went over to the house.

'Come back inside,' she said.

He shook his head.

'If you go to jail you won't see any of them . . . ever again.'

He walked slowly over to the house, head down.

She closed the door behind them.

Good boy.

Just One

SHE MADE IT up.

Only I knew.

She didn't have friends, got invited to parties just 'cause of me. *Tracey & Cheryl* on the envelope, like we were sisters.

Was *so* embarrassing, me carrying the birthday pressie, Cheryl with her bag of food.

'She can't come, it might kill her,' I said, first time we got an invite.

But it wasn't true. She made it up.

When she came to live with us, Mum went on and on 'bout how great it was Cheryl would be in my class at school, I could look out for her. In other words, make sure she didn't eat anything, 'cept what was in her lunch box.

'Nothing from the shop or the school canteen, Tracey, or in friends' houses.'

My friends.

Mum found the party invitation in my pocket when she was washing my uniform.

'Cheryl doesn't want to go,' I said, 'you know, 'cause of . . .'

'Poor wee soul, she feels different from everyone else,' and I got the 'look out' for Cheryl talk again.

'Where's your mum?' I asked.

'Did she get killed by a nut?'

She blinked quick, not letting the tears out.

'Did she lose her magic syringe?'

She stepped back, away from me, her hand going to her school bag.

'Leave her alone.' Kelly-Jo. *My* bestie Kelly-Jo, sticking up for Cheryl. 'Why you always picking on her?' she said, after Cheryl scuttled away.

'She makes it up, 'bout the nut thing.'

Kelly-Jo's eyes widened. '*No* . . . For real? How d'you know, Trace?'

'I . . . seen her eat peanuts.'

Kelly-Jo didn't believe me.

The birthday party was on Saturday. Cheryl said she didn't want to go. I looked at Mum; told you.

'Tracey doesn't want to go on her own.' Mum waited for to me to back her up. I had to say, '*Go on*, come with me.'

Her stupid face lit up.

The party was at McDonald's.

'Cool!' Kelly-Jo liked Cheryl's new rucksack. Inside was her food and her tin box; it went everywhere with her. What if the needle broke? What if she lost the box?

'Want some?' I said to Cheryl, when Kelly-Jo went to the loo.

She shook her head.

'There's no nuts in chips,' I laughed. '*Go on.* Have one.'

She picked up a chip from my plate, looking at it like it was a stick of poison.

I'd been nice to her all day; she didn't want to offend me. She liked it, course she did, better than her boring food.

'*See*, no harm done.'

She smiled.

'Say you ate a nut right now, what would happen?'

Cheryl lost her smile; she looked at her rucksack, making sure it was still beside her chair. 'I'd stop breathing. That's what happened when–'

Kelly-Jo appeared back.

They handed out the birthday cake.

Cheryl looked at the slice on my plate.

'Choccy, yum yum.' I broke off a bit, gave it to her.

'*Trace!* What you doin'?'

'She wants some.'

No reaction to the cake neither, like I knew there wouldn't be. Pretending to be allergic to nuts was to get attention, get people fussing round her. Look at her, huddled up with Kelly-Jo, giggling, her rucksack forgotten; someone could take it, she'd never notice.

Not that she needed it – her tin box with the magic syringe for her pretend allergy.

'Best of three,' said Cheryl. Her and Kelly-Jo were blowing poppers, trying to knock over plastic cups. 'Score!' yelled Cheryl. I slid her rucksack away with my foot, kicked it up the floor under the table.

The look on her face when she seen it was gone! Started gasping, like there was no air. As though she couldn't breathe; same as what she said would happen if she ate nuts.

On her hands and knees, under the table. She found the

bag, checking her magic tin box was still inside, hugging it to her chest, like a teddy.

'If you lost your box could you get another one?'

Panic in her eyes, same way she'd looked in McDonald's when she realised it was gone.

She was good; I had to give her that. Her eyes blinked, holding back tears. *Poor Cheryl. Poor, brave Cheryl.*

'My mum did it . . . injected me last time.'

'D'you think 'bout her all the time?'

She nodded.

'Me too.' It slipped out, 'fore I could stop it.

'Do you know where your mum is?' said Cheryl, her eyes big as saucers.

'Course I do.' I laughed. 'She's downstairs, making the tea.'

I went to the shop. Now, Kelly-Jo would see she was a liar; not the same Cheryl she giggled with 'bout nothing. Not the same Cheryl who made her burst out laughing just by pulling a stupid face.

I wrapped the bag of peanuts in a jumper, hid it in the back of the wardrobe.

'Kelly-Jo's here!' Mum shouted up the stairs.

They were in the kitchen. 'We're making sarnies for a picnic,' said Cheryl, grinning.

'Fab! Back in a sec. I've left something upstairs.'

We headed for the park.

Two free swings. 'Race you!' Kelly-Jo shouted. She made it first; I let Cheryl come second.

I went over to a bench with the rucksack.

Kelly-Jo swung higher than Cheryl, same way she always got higher than me.

'Just one nut could kill me.'

What if it was true? What if she wasn't making it up?

She'd have her magic box.

Cheryl got off the swing, came over. 'Your turn, Tracey.'

She glanced at the rucksack of sarnies. I could feel my cheeks do a redner.

Someone got onto the free swing.

'There's a park behind our house,' said Cheryl, sitting on the bench, hugging her arms round her knees.

'D'you miss your mum?'

'She said she'd come and get me. She always says that.'

We watched Kelly-Jo out-swing everyone. 'I don't like going that high,' said Cheryl, fear in her voice.

She was scared of everything. If I showed her my bag of peanuts she'd probably faint.

'Today, I could eat something with nuts in it.'

My face was on fire.

'Then I'd die.'

'No, you wouldn't, you'd get out your magic syringe.'

'My mum would be glad. She doesn't want me. She never wanted me.'

'Neither did mine.' How'd she do that, make me say things like that, to her of all people?

'Does yours promise she'll come for you?'

Kelly-Jo appeared in front of us. 'Let's have the sarnies. I'm starving.'

I handed them out.

'Mmm, cheese and jam,' said Cheryl, smiling at me, knew it was my fav filling.

She bit into her sandwich.

I held my breath.

She chewed . . . swallowed.

No reaction.

She *did* put it on. I knew it!

'D'you not want that?' said Kelly-Jo, looking at the sandwich in my hand. She'd wolfed hers down.

I took a bite. Now, I could show the bag of peanuts in my pocket to Kelly-Jo; now she'd see that Cheryl–

Ugh! I had jam, cheese and nuts in my mouth.

How could I have mixed up the sandwiches?

'C'mon,' said Kelly-Jo, running back to the swings.

Cheryl watched me throw away the rest of my sarnie for the birds to eat. 'I know you think I'm a pain.'

She brought out her tin box. 'Why do I have to be a freak?' Her eyes filled up. 'I hate it, *hate* this stupid box.'

A bird gobbled up my sandwich. 'Nuts are rotten anyway.'

Cheryl smiled through her tears, as though I'd said, *You're not a freak.*

'C'mon, there's two free swings.'

Cheryl wiped her eyes with her sleeve. 'Race you!'

I gave her a head start, throwing the peanuts for the birds to eat. I kept one though, in case I changed my mind. That's all it would take, after all.

Just one.

Perfect Day

FRIDAY 10TH JUNE. It has rained all week, but today is warm and sunny – a perfect day for a wedding. My suit hangs on the wardrobe door. Is Vanessa lying in bed, gazing at her dress? Did she toss and turn all night, same way I did?

Is she remembering the day we first met, her first day at the office, thinking if she hadn't started working there . . .

Her head was bent over her desk; I couldn't see her face, just her long, dark hair. On my way back from the photocopier she got up from her chair, bumped into me. 'Oh, *sorry*.'

I stared. Knew it was rude, but couldn't stop. She smiled, took it in her stride, would be used to men staring at her.

'First day?' I asked.

She held out her hand. 'Vanessa Ferguson.'

'Mark.' I shook her hand, tried to act normal. 'Mark Caldwell.'

'Could you tell me where the coffee machine is?' she asked. 'I was shown around this morning, but can't remember.'

All the guys tried to hit on her at the start, like I knew they would. I wasn't going to make that mistake. Knew I would get only one chance.

As luck would have it, she walked to work. If it was raining, I offered her a lift home, I was going that direction. After several journeys, she looked more relaxed, sitting beside me in the car, talking about work. Soon, she would invite me in; only a matter of time.

I got lucky again. An Amazon delivery; a large box. I offered to carry it up the steps to her apartment.

She made coffee. Her home was tastefully decorated; paintings, sculptures. I racked my brain for something to talk about other than work.

Bookshelves along the wall. 'You like reading?'

'I'm a bookworm.'

'Me too,' I heard myself say.

Setting down her cup, she went over to the shelves. 'I've just finished the new Hilary Mantel.'

A book the size of a breeze block in her hands. 'Maybe historical fiction's not your thing?'

'No. I mean yes, *absolutely*.'

'Stunning, same as the first one. Would you like to borrow?'

My coffee table almost sagged under it. I knew how it felt. After a fortnight I was at page 28 of 600.

On a wet afternoon, as we walked towards the office car park, she asked what I thought of it. 'Brilliant! The depth of characterisation is remarkable.' I had an online review by heart. 'And the depiction of life at court–' my brother Lenny appeared, coming towards us, out of breath. I had seen him the week before; he'd been complaining about his van over-heating. I knew what he was going to say.

'Mark! Wait up! Can you give us a lift? The van's broke down again.'

We reached Vanessa's apartment, Lenny jabbering in the back seat. He always talked too much. It was embarrassing, Vanessa having to listen to him during the journey. She humoured him, even laughing, as he described his day.

'She's something else, isn't she?' Lenny stuck his head between the two front seats once we were alone. 'D'you have her phone number?'

'As if she would look twice at you.' I laughed at the absurdity of it.

'Why not?'

'For a start, she's a head taller.'

'So?'

'And you're a plumber.'

'So?'

'And you're ugly as sin.'

'Oh, I get it, Mark. *You're* seeing her.' We had reached his house. 'Taking her out tonight?' He closed the car door behind him, laughing, as I swore at him through the glass.

Vanessa came to ask me for a file. She had done something different to her hair, it was wavy, instead of straight.

'I like your hair.'

She hesitated. 'Thanks,' waiting for me to hand over the file.

She must know how I feel, *must* see it in my eyes.

'Vanessa . . .'

'Yes?'

Do it. Just say it. *Would you like to have dinner this weekend? There's a French restaurant . . . The food's unbelievable . . .*

'I need the file later, once you're finished with it.'

When she came back, she seemed to be trying not to laugh out loud. 'Sorry Mark, I'm not laughing at you. I got an email. A story about a fisherman, who has a bet with his best friend he can't live just on fish for ten years.'

Lenny. How did he get her email address?

She was grinning the following day when I walked past her desk. 'Listen to this, Mark . . .'

Okay, so Lenny could mail her his stupid jokes. She found him amusing, that was all. It didn't mean anything. She loved historical fiction, same as me; serious conversation.

We were leaving the office. *Do you like French food, Vanessa? There's a . . .*

'So,' I began. 'Any plans for the weekend?'

Straight hair again, flowing over her shoulders. Her lipstick had worn off to a rim around her lips. I pictured her sitting at her dressing-table mirror in the mornings, in her slip not to smudge her blouse, carefully painting them.

'I've been asked to a children's party.' She smiled. 'A bouncy castle. Jelly and ice cream.'

'Sounds fun.'

Then, it hit me.

'And a clown?'

'So I'm told.'

Lenny was always the star of the show. He used to hire the

outfit, but got so many bookings he bought one. Everyone told him he was wasted as a plumber.

I happened to be walking past the window overlooking the car park one lunchtime. Lenny was leaning against his van. I hadn't arranged to meet him; it wasn't like we ever did lunch.

Vanessa appeared, striding quickly across the car park in her red suit and black high heels, her white blouse flapping in the breeze. Lenny held out his hands as she reached him, taking hers, kissing her – kissing her on the mouth.

She began dropping his name into our conversations in the car. *Lenny was telling me about when you and him . . . That time in school Lenny got you both suspended . . .*

My face smiled; head nodded. Would only be a matter of time until she got bored with him. He was a novelty. That was all.

I overheard her tell a colleague that Lenny was raising money for the new children's hospice. 'Saint Lenny,' I muttered under my breath.

C'mon rain, *please*, I begged a God I didn't believe in . . . Yes! As we drove, I mentioned I was collecting for the Alzheimer's Society on Saturday. 'I need someone to help me, was wondering, if you were free . . .'

It was bloody freezing. Everyone put coins in Vanessa's box instead of mine; all she had to do was smile – a magnet to men, women, kids.

'How often do you do this?' she asked.

'Erm, as often as I can.' It was true, kind of, I gave them a direct debit each month.

Admiration in her eyes, a big smile, just for me.

'Thought we could grab a bite to eat after? There's a–'

Her expression became apologetic. 'Sorry, I've already made plans. Lenny got tickets for the theatre.'

The message light flashed on my answer machine. 'Hey, Mark. How's it going? It's Vanessa's birthday tomorrow. A crowd of us are going out. D'you want to come? Ring me back.'

She kept putting her hand up to her throat during the meal. Wouldn't be a diamond, of course.

'I love your necklace,' someone commented.

Lenny spread his hands. 'Had to sell the van.'

'It'll be a ring next,' another idiot piped up.

I waited for the look of amusement on Vanessa's face, for her to laugh at the ridiculous remark, but she was looking at Lenny, gazing at him, as if none of the rest of us were there.

She wore the necklace every day in work, but that didn't mean anything. She just liked it as a piece of jewellery, that was all.

When I saw Lenny he was like a kid at Christmas, jabbering on about how beautiful Vanessa was, inside as well as out, how he'd never met anyone like her.

I humoured him.

Only a matter of time.

Vanessa helped me with another collection. She said she'd stand at the other entrance, we should raise more that way.

'Already gave to your girlfriend, mate.' I couldn't stop

smiling. Vanessa looked over with a question mark in her eyes. I shook my box. 'Half full!'

She beamed, came across, gave me a hug. 'We make a good team, you and me.'

I had to catch my breath.

Lenny called over to my apartment. Was down in the mouth, not his usual self. He should have known; I felt bad for not warning him he'd get his heart broken. I offered him a drink, would help him drown his sorrows.

His face broke into a grin, as though he couldn't contain it any longer.

I had to congratulate him when he told me. It was like having the air sucked out of your lungs. They'd even set a date. 'Can you believe it, Mark? She's agreed to marry me!' He mock punched my arm. 'Remember you said she wouldn't look twice at me. Huh?'

I had to say yes, when he asked me to be his best man. What else could I say?

Not that it mattered, because there wasn't going to be a wedding.

I stopped at Vanessa's desk before the stag night. 'Just to let you know, I'll take care of Lenny.'

'You'd better!' she laughed. 'No tying him up somewhere, or putting him on a ferry.'

I smiled. 'As if.'

'Take it easy, Mark.' Lenny and the others hadn't finished their drinks; my glass was empty.

'C'mon, what's keeping you?' I thumped him on the back. 'It's your last night as a free man. Get it down you!'

The nightclub filled up. I walked the long way to the bar, scanned the tables . . . They looked suitable – fake-tanned, spilling out of their dresses.

'Hello, ladies. We're on a stag over there. Would you care to join us? Drinks are on me.'

Another couple of double rounds. Lenny was sandwiched between two of the girls. One of them had her arm around him. His head was down, in his hands. I brought my phone out of my pocket. *I'm so sorry Vanessa, I tried to stop him, but he said he wanted to make the most of his last night as a free man . . .*

Look up Lenny, smile for the camera.

'Yuk!' The girls jumped up from their seats. Lenny was throwing up. A bouncer came over, asked us to leave.

Friday 10th June. It has rained all week, but today is warm and sunny – a perfect day for a wedding. My suit hangs on the wardrobe door. The phone is ringing. It clicks onto the machine.

'Mark! Where are you? Why are you not answering your mobile? You'd better not still be in bed. You're meant to be here! Pick up the phone. It's my wedding day, remember! *Wake UP!*

He runs out of his house as I pull up, gesturing frantically at me. 'Don't get out of the car. There's a problem at the florist's; they can't deliver, you need to pick them up.'

Vanessa's mother answers the doorbell. The bridesmaids fuss over the flowers.

'I need to see Vanessa.'

'You can't,' her mother begins. 'Of course, you can. It's only bad luck to see the groom.'

She turns her head at the sound of the bedroom door opening. Her dress shimmers in the sunlight through the window. One of the curls piled on top of her head has fallen down.

'Mark.' She floats towards me.

Another step, and she'll be in my arms.

'Oh, Mark,' she laughs, taking my hands in hers. 'Look at me. I can't stop smiling.'

'You're very pale.' She indicates to sit on the bed. 'Has Lenny got you running around after him?'

At the dressing-table, she pins the stray curl back up with the rest. Tiny freckles on the backs of her arms. I am close enough to touch them, to trace my fingers along the perfect skin.

'Have to pull myself together.' She makes a serious face at herself in the mirror. 'I'll never get make-up on at this rate.'

'You don't need any.'

She reaches over, places her hand on mine.

'I know men find it hard to talk about their feelings . . .'

I can't breathe. She knows I love her.

'Lenny thinks the world of you. He got this silly idea in his head that you didn't want to be his best man. He was very upset. It means a lot to him.'

How can she not see it in my eyes? How can she not know how I feel?

'I'd never have met him, if it wasn't for you.'

'Vanessa . . .'

I love you. I have loved you since the first day I met you.

It wouldn't make any difference. She'll still love Lenny. Still marry Lenny.

'What is it, Mark?'

I shake my head. 'You don't want to know.'

Her brow bunches.

'Have to go.'

'Mark?'

I tell myself to stand, to walk to the door. My mouth opens and words come out, 'There are videos . . . on his phone.'

She waits for me to explain.

'Of kids.'

She grins. 'They love him. He's so wonderful with them. Even without the clown,' she sees the expression on my face, her voice faltering, '. . . outfit.'

'My loyalty should be to Lenny. But, we're such good friends, you and me.'

Her face pales.

'I confronted him. He denied it, gave me his phone, said, "Show me." He'd deleted them.'

'*Videos* . . . ?' Her voice trembles.

'Him and . . . boys.'

She can't take it in, gazes blankly at me.

Her eyes fill.

Brim.

A huge tear spills, makes its way down her cheek. She is thinking – I can see in her eyes, as clearly as if she says it. *That's why you didn't want to be his best man . . . That's why he's always around children . . .*

She stands, goes to step one way, then the other, blind with shock.

I take her in my arms.

Our reflection in the dressing-table mirror – a bride with her groom.

Her tears soak into my suit; she shudders with each sob. I stroke the back of her neck, silken skin under my fingertips.

A curl of hair escapes its pin.

I watch it cascade in the mirror.

Sunlight streams through the window, illuminating us.

Would have been a perfect day, for a wedding.

'Bad Boy' Blade

NORMAN LOOKED AROUND his new garden. Moving house was a stressful experience. Downsizing, as Doreen called it, but this could hardly be called a garden. A tiny square of grass, a few brown and lifeless-looking shrubs, and one miserable flower bed.

Picturing his old garden almost brought a tear to Norman's eye – the cherry blossom over the patio, where he caught forty winks on sunny afternoons, a place of refuge while Doreen gave the house a going over in her daily cleaning attack. She was unpacking boxes, after making up her bed. That was another sore point about this terrible moving ordeal – *his* bed. The furniture removal men hadn't brought it yet. He didn't need this stress at his age!

'*Norman?* Where are you?'

Could she not give him five minutes to himself?

Doreen tutted loudly. 'Where has he got to now?'

Norman stayed where he was, behind a shrub. She called again from the back door, louder, not wanting to come into the garden in her slippers. She would get fed up and go back inside in a minute.

Another female voice; high pitched, unfamiliar.

He peeked around the bush. Doreen was talking over the garden fence to a tall, thin-faced woman. 'Sorry, I didn't mean to disturb you.'

'Are you looking for your husband?' asked the woman.

'Norman is my dog,' replied Doreen.

Norman waited for the woman's laugh. How could it still get to him so much after all these years? It was just a name, he had told himself in his darker hours. The times in the park were the hardest to bear. Doreen loved to play 'throw the ball'. It made her so happy that Norman pretended it was his favourite, too. She danced about, waving the ball in the air, faking to throw it. When she finally let go, Norman hurtled across the grass, but Doreen would already be shouting at the top of her voice, '**Fetch, Norman!**' At which every dog's head turned in his direction, some with sneering glances, others smiling with amusement.

As a puppy, Doreen had cradled him in her arms. 'Wee Norman,' she cooed. Norman had pricked up his ears, but he was not mistaken. Norman had been her late father's name, he afterwards discovered.

The conversation at the fence seemed to be over; the tall woman walked towards her house. Norman scooted up the garden past Doreen, almost tripping her up.

Doreen tutted as she closed the back door after them. 'Norman, *what* is wrong with you? Why were you hiding?'

Norman trotted to the corner of the kitchen (where his bed should have been), lying down.

'It'll turn up. If it doesn't, I'll buy you–'

The doorbell rang.

The tall woman from next door held a teapot in her hand. 'A spare one,' she said. Doreen switched on the kettle.

'Oh, this is Norman, then?' The woman studied him for several moments. 'Jack Russells are such cute little dogs.'

Norman put his chin on his paws, closed his eyes in disgust.

'Norman, come and say hello to Hilda.'

He pretended to be asleep.

'He's usually very friendly,' Doreen apologised. 'But he's not himself at the minute. The move seems to have unsettled him. The removal men have misplaced his bed.'

Norman inwardly sighed, pictured the teeth marks on the edge of the blue rubber side where he'd chewed it at that tender age when he didn't know better.

'They say moving house is one of the most stressful things you can do,' said Doreen.

Norman opened an eye. Tell him about it!

'That, and changing job, or divorce,' said Hilda.

'Neither of those apply to me,' said Doreen. 'I'm a retired spinster.'

'If you can move house and only lose a teapot and a dog bed, I think you are doing very well!'

Doreen nodded, but looked anxiously at Norman.

'Don't worry about him. Pets sulk over the slightest thing. When I think of the times Blade . . .'

Norman's ears pricked up. *Blade?* That was a name and a half! Oh boy, what he would give for a name like that.

'Has sulked with me. Wouldn't come near me or speak to me for days. Just because I gave him a bath.'

'What breed is he?' asked Doreen.

Hilda looked confused. 'He's not a dog.'

As long as it's not a cat, thought Norman.

'He's a parrot.'

'Great company,' Hilda went on, extolling the virtues of a bird that learned to talk *incredibly* quickly. (Repeating words, how clever was that?) Apparently, it went outside, flew round the garden and came back in, never flew away. (Definitely thick as a stick, Norman decided.)

'I'd be lost,' Hilda sighed, 'without my Blade.'

Doreen smiled and nodded, but wasn't so kindly disposed to Blade at six o'clock the following morning, when loud squawking woke her and Norman.

The same happened every day that week.

They went round next door.

'An early bird!' trilled Hilda, inviting Doreen and Norman in.

'Here's the culprit,' she smiled, indicating a large cage. 'Blade's a bad boy, isn't he?'

'**Bad Boy! Bad Boy!**' yelled the ugly green bird inside.

'Does it, I mean *he*, always waken so early?'

'Once it's light he's up and ready for his breakfast. I tried putting a sheet over his cage, but he didn't like it. Screamed the house down all night.'

Doreen looked at Norman. He knew what she was thinking – something would have to be done about the bird.

Norman's opportunity came that afternoon.

He was in the garden, stretching his legs, when he noticed Blade perched on an open window of next door. The bird cocked its head, staring back at Norman, the red streak down its face glinting in the sunshine.

Norman pretended to sniff the soil in the flower bed.

Before long, Blade seemed to forget all about him, flying across his garden, landing on the dividing fence.

'**Hi Mum!**'

Norman gave a start, glancing around, but no one else was there.

He moved slowly, not to startle the bird, which was jabbering to itself, edging closer . . . closer still. Was just about to spring up the fence and seize Blade by the throat when *he* came under attack – the fury with which an impossibly sharp beak swooped on Norman, battering his body as he ran for cover towards his back door was matched by the incessant shrieking from the bird, as if *it* was the one running for *its* life.

Doreen and Hilda came hurrying out.

Hilda blamed Norman.

Doreen blamed Blade.

It all got very messy, with the end result being a hastily returned teapot.

There were no more chats over the fence, and poor Norman no longer felt safe in his own garden. Even inside, he was sure he could hear his name being mockingly chanted amongst the racket coming through the wall.

Doreen tried to find a solution to her early morning wake-up call by purchasing earmuffs.

'**Keep quiet!**' The very house seemed to shake with the screech.

Doreen spoke loudly, so that Norman, at the other end of the duvet, could hear her above the din. 'Enough is enough!'

Norman waited for her to jump out of bed, rush round next door to give Hilda what for. She didn't move though. In fact, she was sitting very still with a strange expression on her face.

'There is a well-known saying, Norman. *Attack is the best form of defence.*'

Norman wasn't convinced, knew the pitfalls of this theory from his terrible experience with Blade in the garden.

'We are going to play them at their own game.'

We? Norman was getting worried.

'Hilda goes to bed early. If she doesn't care about our lack of sleep, why should we care about hers?'

Doreen didn't further explain, and that night Norman waited in trepidation for what 'the plan' would entail for him. When the hands of the mantelpiece clock reached eleven, Doreen got up from her chair.

Norman held his breath, but all she did was walk over to the record player. He got a surprise when the music started. His favourite – 'Sing-Along with Des'. Doreen hadn't played it in ages. There was nothing Norman liked better than a good singalong. The tunes were so catchy he could never resist joining in.

Hilda didn't appreciate Des and Norman's duet. In fact, she was extremely upset by the 'intolerable racket' every night.

Doreen nodded sympathetically each time Hilda came round to complain about her awful migraines brought on by lack of sleep. The move had unsettled Norman, Doreen explained. She was trying to cheer him up, he'd always had a thing about Des O'Connor . . .

The doorbell rang one afternoon.

A man from the council on the doorstep. Hilda had complained about noise pollution. It had been recorded, was above the acceptable level in a residential area at night-time. Doreen's face turned a strange purple colour. 'And what about that?!' Blade's piercing trill could be heard through the wall. 'Is *that* acceptable?'

To Norman's disappointment, there were no more singalongs.

He didn't like being woken at an unearthly hour each morning either, but it seemed there was nothing they could do.

Doreen looked thoughtful; stared into space.

To Norman's astonishment, she began making a cake.

She never baked.

'C'mon, Norman,' she said, when the cake had cooled. 'A peace offering,' she added, as they waited for Hilda to answer the door.

Thankfully, Blade was in his cage. Norman lay down beside Doreen's chair, out of sight, so the bird couldn't stare at him with those awful beady eyes. Hilda smiled, telling Doreen she no longer took migraines. Doreen said she was very glad to hear it.

Doreen looked over at Blade's cage, asking Hilda about him, where she had got him, what he liked to eat . . . When Hilda went to refill the teapot, Doreen caught Norman's eye; winked.

What was she playing at?

The sound of Hilda's car driving away the next morning.

Doreen rushed over to the window.

She opened the back door, going into the garden. Norman sat on the doorstep, not going further because Blade was perched on the dividing fence.

'Hello, Blade. Who's a lovely boy then?'

Norman shook his head, must have something lodged in his ears, couldn't be hearing right. Doreen put her hand in her apron pocket. 'Your favourite, Blade.'

The bird cocked its head, studying what she had dropped on the ground. Flying down from the fence, it picked up the grape in its beak.

In a flash, Doreen had thrown her cardigan over him, wrapped him up in it. Norman expected the bird to yell blue murder, but he must have been stunned into silence.

Doreen quickly bundled him into her car boot, sped off.

Norman retreated into the house and hid under the kitchen table.

He felt sick, his paws trembling, was worse than going to the vet's, waiting for the sound of Hilda's car returning, finding Blade gone. Norman couldn't get his head around what he'd just witnessed, but there you go, you could live with someone all your life and they could still shock you.

'*Norman?* Where are you?'

Doreen was back.

He crept from below the table.

'Listen to that, Norman.'

Norman pricked an ear. Couldn't hear anything.

'Exactly,' said Doreen.

A few minutes later, the sound of a car outside. Hilda, heavy on the brakes, as usual.

Norman retreated back under the table.

Doreen hummed to herself, put on the kettle.

Norman cringed. Hilda's voice outside, calling for Blade.

The doorbell rang.

'H-have you seen Blade?' Hilda was so distraught she could barely speak. Norman pressed his chin on his paws, tried to stop their tremble. No, Doreen had been cleaning all morning, hadn't been outside. Norman couldn't believe what he was hearing, the lies slipping off her tongue.

'I'm sure he'll show up, must have fancied a change of scenery.' Doreen glanced in Norman's direction, under the table, as if he were a conspirator!

'Where's Norman?' asked Hilda.

Her head appeared under the table. He tried to put on his most innocent expression and not shake, not alert her something untoward had been going on.

'He's been inside with me all morning,' said Doreen. 'Sit down and have a cup of tea.' No, Hilda didn't want tea, had to keep looking . . .

She came back later, wringing her hands, eyes red-rimmed. There was no sign of him, anywhere! 'I'm sure he'll turn up tomorrow,' said Doreen.

They helped Hilda search the town, the park. Doreen even said, 'He'll be perched on one of the trees, just you wait and see.' They helped put up posters: *Have you seen my Blade?*

Hilda was a wreck, wore the same clothes each day;

Norman's nose twitched. It was her fault, she sobbed to Doreen, leaving the window open when not there, would never forgive herself!

Now guilt would overcome Doreen. Norman waited for her to exclaim: It was me. I can't live with myself any longer!

'Have another cup of tea,' said Doreen.

He was living with a psychopath.

Norman went into the garden, to stretch his legs.

A large brown bird was perched on the fence. Seemed to be asleep, its head under its wing, but must have sensed Norman's presence, its head appearing.

Time stood still. Norman recognised him, despite his dirty, bedraggled state, would know those beady eyes anywhere.

Shrieking!

Hilda, at her window.

Doreen came outside to see what all the fuss was about. Struggled to arrange her face into a pleased smile, looked like she'd a biscuit stuck in her throat.

Blade no longer went outside.

There were no more early morning wake-up calls.

Hilda was consulting a parrot psychologist; Blade had post-traumatic stress disorder, would come round, she had been assured, would take time, but should get back to his old self. Doreen had to nod and say, 'Hopefully' – shared a look with Norman – *not*. Norman didn't feel too hot himself, after all the goings-on, but was cheerful in front of Doreen, didn't want her getting a shrink for *him*.

The empty house on the other side of Doreen and Norman's was sold. Doreen woke Norman from his nap as she clattered in the back door. 'Such *lovely* people,' she enthused, telling him about their new neighbours.

'And thank heavens no birds. *Definitely not*,' she laughed. 'You should see their cat. He's enormous! They say he's friendly, just looks ferocious.'

Norman inwardly sighed; pictured Blade sitting on the fence before swooping down on him.

There was another well-known saying.

Better the devil you know.

Scar

THIS IS MY office. My desk. Through the window behind me is my view over the city.

My office; my desk; my view.

A tall man brought me up here. 'Great to have you back, Christine.'

I walked over to the large window behind the desk.

'Wish my office had your view.'

My eyes scanned the city, looking for something, anything, familiar.

'Catch you later,' he said.

I sat at the desk, fumbling for the notebook in my handbag, writing the words before I forgot them:

My office
My desk
My view

This is what I do. I come here each day, sit at this desk. I slide out a drawer. Inside are blue folders. They contain pages with numbers in boxes; words – Tax Deductions; Capital Allowances; Net Profit.

I lift a pen from the pot on the desk, hold it over a page. This is what I do. If I look at the page for long enough, it will come back to me. That is why I am here. My neurologist thinks it might help jog my memory. I don't recognise anything though, not the room, not the people who spoke to me on my way to this office. 'Welcome back, Christine . . . How are you?'

I no longer have physical injuries from the accident, just the ones inside my head that have taken away my memory. I can remember my childhood, my teenage years, up to my last year at school. After that – nothing. My neurologist says this is common with head trauma. I don't remember things that have happened since the accident either. Like being in hospital. Instead, the vivid recollection of falling off my bike when I was nine, breaking my arm; the children's ward, how itchy it got under the plaster.

I keep losing time as well; what seems like minutes is really hours. I can be thinking about something for a moment, realise an hour has passed on my watch.

How did I get here? The question jumps into my mind. I close my eyes, concentrating . . . My husband brought me, in his car. He wanted to accompany me inside, but I said I was okay on my own. I can't remember his name – a flurry of panic rushes through me – I reach for my notebook.

My name is Christine Hepworth
My husband is Neil Hepworth
Our daughter is called Ruby

Ruby. How can I keep forgetting about Ruby? Neil puts her into my arms and I study this child I'm told is mine. She gazes back at me, eyes widening, as if she also doubts we know each other. She doesn't want to stay in my arms; Neil lifts her into the air, swings her round; she squeals with delight.

He takes my hand to show me something. Points to paintings, explains where we got them; describes the holidays we brought them back from, smiling and shaking his head, I made him spend all our time in galleries. A photograph on a shelf – he tells me about our wedding day, buying our house, Ruby's birth, and I nod, as though it's starting to come back to me. I can't tell him I have no recollection of any of it. Can't tell him the last thing I remember is being at school, with a crush on the head boy.

A knock on the door. I hurriedly close the notebook, my pen poised over the page from the blue folder.

A woman comes into the room. She holds up the paper bag in her hands. 'Lunch.'

How can it be lunchtime already?

She reaches me a plastic bowl of salad and a bag of crisps. 'Prawn cocktail, your favourite,' she says. I stare at the crisps. I don't know what my favourite foods are. I fumble for a tissue in my handbag, blow my nose. I can't burst into tears.

She sits on the chair at the other side of the desk, opens her bowl of salad, picks at it with a fork.

Do I usually have lunch with her? I wonder.

'What is your name?'

She looks up from her salad, her expression shocked, covers it with a smile. 'Zoe.'

I open my bowl of salad. *Is it one of my favourite foods as well?* 'I don't remember anything,' I hear myself confiding. 'About here . . . about my life.'

A sudden need to tell her. I open my notebook, flick through the pages until I find what the neurologist called it.

'I've got retrograde amnesia.'

'What does that mean?' she asks.

There is no explanation in my notebook.

'I can't remember.'

Her eyes are sympathetic.

'I can't remember what's wrong with my memory.'

It's funny when I say it out loud. Absurd. I burst out laughing; she hesitates, then joins in.

'You haven't forgotten your sense of humour,' she says.

We are friends, I'm sure we are, not just work colleagues.

'Do we usually have lunch together?'

She nods. 'We sometimes go to a nearby café.'

'What do you do here?' I ask, hoping for a clue to what I do.

'I'm an accountant, same as you.'

She glances at the blue folder on my desk. 'All your files, and everything you need to know about your clients will be on your laptop.'

Laptop?

I turn my attention to opening my bag of crisps, so she doesn't see that I don't understand what she is talking about.

'Have you met . . .'

I look again at my notebook.

Accident
Hospital
Retrograde amnesia

'My husband?'

'Yes, I've met Neil.'

Neil – I must remember his name.

'And Ruby,' she adds.

Ruby! I have a daughter called Ruby.

'Am I happy . . . Am I happy with Neil?'

She hesitates; I must sound bizarre. 'You seem so . . . Yes.'

I have so much to ask, but she glances at her watch. 'I've a client at two. Better go.'

'Thank you for lunch,' I say, as she reaches the door. She turns back, smiles, closes the door behind her.

I lift my pen, flick to a new page in my notebook.

Zoe
Accountant
Happy

I eat a crisp.

Prawn cocktail crisps

It can take time for memories to come back, according to my neurologist. Patience is important. I look at the page from the folder again, the columns of numbers. The words mean nothing to me – VAT; Gross Profit; Allowable Expenses. I pick up my pen, poising it over the page . . .

I am exhausted. I lean back in my chair, closing my eyes, picture Zoe's face. (I remembered her name!)

She said I am happy. I picture my husband's face; the concern in his eyes when he looks at me. I must love him. We are married. I must love him. He holds my face between his hands, kisses me gently, as if I am fragile, as if I might break. 'We almost lost you.' His eyes glisten. He loves me. I must love him.

What if my memories never come back? I asked my neurologist. (I can remember *neurologist*, but not her name.) She said everyone is different, some people regain the lost years, others don't. 'Best not to focus on that, Christine. Take each day slowly, try to help your brain make new memories by jotting down notes, taking photographs.' Photographs! I bring my phone out of my bag. It is called a mobile. (I remembered the name!) My husband showed me how to take photographs with it. I take one of the desk, the folder, the pen pot, a picture on the wall.

The view.

A knock on the door.

The tall man, who brought me up here this morning. Perhaps it is time to go home.

He comes over to stand beside me at the window.

Gazes at me, as if waiting for me to speak.

He puts his hand on my arm.

'Missed you.'

His fingers squeeze.

'So much, babe.'

My husband asks about my day. 'I had lunch with . . .' I open my notebook. 'Zoe.'

He smiles. 'Same as usual then.'

'Do you know the others at my work?'

'I've met some of them.'

'Do you know . . .' But what can I say? *Do you know Tall?*

Our daughter comes over to us, reaches up her arms to be lifted. I go to do it, but she draws back, doesn't want me, I can see in her eyes she is thinking – who are you?

'Who am I?'

My husband's face is stricken.

'What type of person, I mean?' *Am I the type of person who has an affair?*

He puts his hand on his chin. 'Kind, thoughtful, good fun. Hmm . . .' He lifts our daughter. 'Headstrong. Untidy. Mummy's always leaving her clothes on the floor, isn't she Ruby?' He nods at Ruby; she nods back. He laughs; Ruby laughs. They don't need me; they are happy together, on their own. Is that why I am having an affair? Because no one needs me at home?

I try to hold back tears.

He shifts Ruby to one arm, puts his other around me. Ruby turns away her face, starts to fret.

'She's just getting used to having you back,' he says in bed that night. 'It'll take time, Christine, that's all.' He kisses me, gently. 'Love you.'

My office

My desk
My view

Folders in drawer. 'Don't try to force a memory,' my neurologist said. 'Follow your usual routine, let your brain recognise for you what is happening, go with the flow.' I take a pen from the pot. Gaze at a page . . . *Add expenses column. Take away this figure from gross profit* – it is coming back to me! Can't wait to tell Neil. I remembered his name!

I turn the page, add up another column.

A knock on the door.

Tall.

'I'm busy,' but he has already closed the door, is beside me, hunkered down.

'You *really* don't know me?'

I shake my head.

'Oh, babe.' He takes my face between his hands, like my husband does.

'I'm married.'

'In name only.'

I pull away his hands.

'You're leaving him, to be with me.'

'No!'

He tries to kiss me; I turn my head, his lips graze my cheek, I put my hands against his chest; push.

'I know, going too fast, rushing you.' He puts up his palms in mock defence. 'It's just I've missed you, babe . . . missed *us*.'

He goes over to the door. Looks back. Blows me a kiss.

I can no longer concentrate on the columns of numbers.

In name only.

Is this why Neil never wants to make love?

Another knock on the door.

What if it's him again?

It opens.

The woman I have lunch with.

I flick through my notebook.

Zoe

Accountant

Happy

She said I was happily married!

As we eat, I describe him to Zoe. 'Tall, fair hair . . .'

'Good looking? Loud ties?'

I nod.

'Sounds like Gavin.'

I write his name in my notebook.

'What about him?' asks Zoe.

'Do I like him?'

She laughs; I must sound bizarre again. 'Yeah, think so. Why?'

I'm having an affair with him, I almost say, but don't want Zoe to think badly of me. She's met . . . I flick back in my notebook. Neil and Ruby.

'This morning I remembered . . .'

Zoe leans forward, eager to hear.

I point at the blue folder. 'Capital gains.'

'Ah.'

She sees I'm disappointed by her reaction. 'It's just . . . It's boring.' She gazes at the folder. 'Accountancy. We're both bored to tears.'

I write it down.

Bored

Accountancy

Tears

'I shouldn't have said that. It's great you remembered; it really is!' She looks at her watch. 'Have to go, I've a meeting, catch you later,' and she leaves with her lunch half eaten.

Neil says, 'Let's get a takeaway.' He hands me a menu. 'Do I like Chinese food?' He nods. 'Your favourite is Indian, we can order that instead if–' 'No, it's fine, you pick something for me.' 'The hotter the better then,' he laughs.

He is good fun, kind, generous, loving, a wonderful father; how can I be having an affair? *You're leaving him.* Does that mean I'm leaving my daughter as well? Could I be this person?

The front door closes behind him. Ruby is playing on the floor, trying to balance a wooden block on top of another. I go over to the photograph on the shelf, gaze at my lace dress; the roses in my hands; my face; the joy in my eyes.

A sound.

I glance behind . . . she's not there!

The blocks are piled high on the floor.

But I only turned my back for a moment. Ruby? I rush into the kitchen. *Ruby?* The hall, the bathroom, the bedrooms,

Ruby! Fear flooding me. Sudden clarity – love; my love for her, I would die for my child, I have felt this panic before. Know where she is.

I lie on the bedroom carpet, turn my head to below the bed. Point a finger, found you! She smiles, giggles; we lock eyes; she crawls out, into my arms, knows something has changed in me.

We are still wrapped together when Neil comes back, the sound of the front door opening and closing. He calls our names. I put my finger to my lips to tell Ruby we are both hiding. We giggle when he calls into each room, when he can't find us. 'Ah ha! What are my two favourite ladies doing in here, may I ask?'

I go to say, to tell him, but he already knows, is on the carpet beside us, drawing us to him, rocking us in his arms, his tears soaking into my hair.

My office

I lock the door.
Open the desk drawer.
Blue folder.
Knocking.
'Who is it?'
I don't let him in.
Whizz down columns; smiling.
Another knock on the door. I look at my watch.
'What's with the security?'
'Hello, Zoe.'

She claps.

I point at myself. 'Christine.' At my wedding band, oh no, I can't . . . 'Neil!' I make a cradle with my arms. 'Ruby.' I look around for something else. Zoe points at the folder on the desk.

'Boring.'

We burst into laughter.

'Your turn,' I say, realising I haven't asked anything about her, I've been so wrapped up in myself.

I point at her wedding band.

In my notebook I write the names of her husband and two sons.

She points at the blue folder. 'Early retirement.'

We burst out laughing again.

Why have my feelings for Ruby returned, but not for Neil? We are like flatmates, best friends, not husband and wife.

I put Ruby to bed, take his hand, lead him into our bedroom. Unbutton his shirt . . . He undresses me, asks am I sure? He hadn't wanted to rush me, that was why we haven't . . .

We lie on the bed; his lips move down my throat, on down . . . I close my eyes; it is . . . pleasant . . . more than that, will be in a moment . . .

I draw him back up, my lips against his, trying to match the urgency in his kiss, in his body moving against mine. I picture the photograph on the shelf, willing our wedding night to come back to me. He is almost there; I grip tighter to his back, willing myself. I speak his name, 'Neil, Neil,' I can get there too, I can . . . I can.

A knock on my office door.

I point to the chair at the other side of the desk.

'How long have we been together?' I ask.

He adjusts his tie; smiles. 'Over a year.'

'Where?'

'Pardon?'

'Where do we meet?'

'You come to my apartment.'

My eyes move to his lips; is this the reason I feel no passion with my husband?

He locks the door, comes round the desk, embraces me.

If I kiss him, I'll know. It will prove I'm having an affair, if I feel it with him . . . At the last moment I can't, turn my head.

His lips on my neck, hands roaming over me. I feel a stirring . . . sort of. *Do I?* He unbuttons my blouse; seems very practised, assured, as though he's done this with lots of women, his fingers on my bra straps, sliding them . . . I stop him. 'I've kissed every centimetre of you, Christine.'

'Where is my scar?'

His eyes move to my temple.

'The old one. The one I got when I fell off my bike, when I was a child.'

'I'm hardly gonna notice a little scar,' he laughs.

'There was glass on the road.'

His eyes flick away, towards the view.

'Your back.'

He reads my face. '*C'mon*, it doesn't mean . . .'

I point to the door.

Lunchtime.

Zoe hasn't her usual paper carrier. 'The walls are closing in!' She grimaces. 'Let's go out for lunch.'

In the café, I want to tell her, ask should I report him, but what if she thinks badly of me, thinks I encouraged him.

The waitress comes over. 'What's the soup today?' asks Zoe.

'Roast tomato and chilli. A warning, ladies: it's heavy on the chilli.'

I love spicy food – I remember Neil saying! Everything will be fine at home; it will just take time. I picture his sweet face.

'Wow!' says Zoe, after tasting the soup. 'She wasn't joking!'

I raise an eyebrow – not hot at all.

Zoe laughs.

She reaches for her water glass, 'On fire here!'

There is something about the way she waves her hand up and down in front of her mouth – a sudden recollection, of being here before, the smell of chilli . . . My memory must be playing tricks.

I set down my spoon.

A trick. *Must be.* I can't trust my memory.

Hear myself saying, 'I fell off my bike when I was nine.'

Zoe stills.

'It left a scar.'

A trick of memory, that's all. Not true.

'Your hip.'

We gaze at each other.

There is nothing to say. Everything has already been said.

I'm not leaving Neil because I can't do it to him, I still love him, just not in that way. I can't do it to him, or to Ruby.

Zoe is prepared to give up her family.

We sit. Food forgotten. The waitress comes over, says something . . . moves away again.

Love, longing, guilt, reflected back to me in Zoe's eyes.

Waiting

THE HAG SAT outside her hut.

'Halloa! What is your rush, young friend?' she hollered, as Ludwig hurried past, hoping not to be noticed.

'I . . . I . . . er,' said Ludwig, a youth of few words, yet fine features, as the hag had been quick to note.

'Could you spare a moment, just a moment, my fine fellow, to help a poor lady? Ah, I see you don't think me a lady. You don't think my dress dandy,' she plucked at the rag she had on, 'or my locks luscious,' tossing her matted mane, which trailed on the ground, over one shoulder.

'I . . . er . . . you said *help*?' replied Ludwig, still eager to be on his way, yet not unkind.

The hag smiled, large mouthed and toothless. Ludwig thought of tunnels. 'A brawny beast, that's what I need,' said the hag. 'A brawny beast like yourself, to open . . .' And she delved into the depths of her foul rag, brought out a bottle, shook it at him.

'I . . . er . . . of course,' said Ludwig, who prided himself on his bulging biceps, and could spare a moment to help a hag.

He reached for the bottle in her hand, startled by the green eye on the hag's knobbled knuckle.

'Just a ring, sweet sonny,' said the hag, but the pupil of the eye moved, watching Ludwig, he was sure it did, and he hurried to release the bottle cork, so he could continue on his way.

Despite his mighty muscles, it would not be coaxed. 'Those perfect pearlies you have there, my lovely laddie,' said the hag, 'will have it out in a jiffy.'

Ludwig lifted the bottle to his mouth, clamped on the cork with his manly molars.

Woosh, out came the cork.

A few droplets of the bottle's contents touched his lips.

Such divine dew he had never tasted, he *must* have more, *glug, glug, glug* . . . the bottle was dry, and everything around Ludwig began getting bigger and bigger, or maybe he was shrinking, getting smaller and smaller. A large black tunnel opened in front of him; he tried to run away, but the tunnel sucked him in; he was tumbling down and down in vile-smelling darkness.

The hag sat outside her hut.

Tucked away the bottle under her wretched rag.

Waited for the next Ludwig.

Pinter Genes

HAROLD JOHN PINTER'S luck had run out.

The realisation filled him with despair. But he didn't complain, or rail at his fate.

It had been inevitable.

He came from a line of unfortunates. Bad luck ran in the Pinter genes, in the same way other families inherited aquiline noses or quick tempers. Harold John found it interesting (before, not now) that just prior to their downfall his predecessors often experienced great success or triumph.

Take for example his great grandfather. He had been the inventor of the paper clip. A clock maker by trade, he didn't realise he needed to patent it, was extremely shocked to hear it was his lifelong friend who was behind this ingenious new device. It wasn't the large fortune made by his 'friend' which instigated his slow, but steady decline through alcohol into an early grave, but the betrayal of his trust. As a teenager, Harold John was told of poor Great Grandfather's misfortune when being warned of the perils of alcohol.

John Pinter, Harold John's grandfather, didn't make the

same mistake of trusting those around him. He was reportedly a solitary man by nature, with a passion for long-distance running. In fact, he seemed to have an obsession for the sport. Some might say it was to forget his mundane job at the linen mill, or perhaps to escape from his sharp-tongued wife awaiting the arrival of their fourth offspring. Whatever the reason, he diligently trained and won every cross-country event in the county, becoming a local celebrity.

But this triumph was short-lived, as he was stopped in his tracks by 'another woman' (a second peril warning for the young Harold John). Though it wasn't strictly true to say that she stopped him; rather, it was her spouse, who paid Grandfather Pinter a surprise visit, knocking him across the parlour floor towards the fireplace, on the hearth of which he unluckily fell and split his head, leaving Grandmother Pinter to bring up their new infant Harold on her own.

Most might assume that Harold John's father would have heeded the mistakes of his elders, but he threw caution to the wind, combining the perils of alcohol and loose women, opening a 'drinking establishment' with his 'lady friend', Sadie. Contrary to Pinter tradition, Harold didn't show promise in any particular field before sliding into disrepute and ending up at Her Majesty's hospitality for allowing consumption of alcohol and card games after hours and not paying his taxes.

Whilst inside, he found himself being visited by a charitable woman (and his wife-to-be), Harold John's mother, who was temporarily performing the Reverend Morrow's duties (whilst he was on a six-month sabbatical), explaining the path to redemption to the corrupt and lost members of society.

Harold John's father at first paid scant attention to this plain, mousy-haired young woman sitting on the other side of the visiting table, until one day, having dropped a cigarette onto the floor, and reached under the table to retrieve it, he noticed a very shapely pair of ankles, demure above flat lace-up shoes, but somehow exciting after Sadie's thick calves and red high heels.

Harold John to this day had no idea how his mother ended up marrying his father on his release. It was impossible to fathom how he could have persuaded her to make such an unsuitable match.

The marriage appeared to get off to a good start, but shortly before the birth of Harold John, his father seemed to tire of his new steady job in the foundry, or maybe he grew bored of the constant clack of his wife's knitting needles as booties, cardigans and so on were lovingly produced for her imminent baby.

He began taking late-night walks, to stretch his legs before bedtime. These soon developed into *after* bedtime walks, slipping out once his wife was asleep. Being a small, slim man, windows were usually easy for him to squeeze through. The silver was seldom locked away; it looked so much nicer on display on the dining room table. He had many profitable walks, until the master of one house was downstairs in the early hours for a glass of water, when in through the kitchen window fell the hapless Harold, almost at his feet.

It seemed to be becoming a Pinter tradition for fathers to be absent from their children's lives, as after serving his sentence – again with his wife sitting (red-eyed and strained this time) across the visiting table, clutching Harold

John so tightly to her breast she almost suffocated him – he disappeared.

Never to this day having contacted Harold John. Not that Harold John minded. He liked his solitary existence, his job as bank clerk during the day, nights alone in his small bedsit, which he usually spent reading. There were few variations to this routine, except visits to see his mother, who was pleased to see he had turned out well (unlike you-know-who). Fortunately, for Harold John, the only similarity between himself and his father seemed to be his favouring of a walk through the town each evening before turning in. The fresh air helped him sleep.

His life was uneventful, the way he liked it. And things would probably have remained like that, if one day two men hadn't burst into the bank, demanding the money in the safe from Harold John, who was totalling a ledger with the manager. They had a gun, so Harold John did as he was told, opening the safe and handing over the contents.

The two villains were making a hasty exit when the bank manager couldn't seem to bear the loss of the safe money and dived for the robber's gun, trying to wrestle it from him. The other robber made a run for it. Surprisingly, especially to Harold John himself, Harold John ran after him, giving chase through the town, eventually catching up and hurling him to the ground.

Harold John became a hero. In the tussle for the gun the bank manager had been shot, and although the bullet was carefully removed, he died a few days later. His assailant had escaped with the bag of money, but due to Harold's John heroic chase, the other robber was brought to justice and imprisoned.

Harold John found himself the toast of the town. Men who had not formerly acknowledged him in the bank now tipped their hats to him in the street, and it surprised no one that he was asked to take over as manager, moving into the grand living accommodation above the bank. Moreover, as is often the case, his new-found success in life brought a further source of happiness. This took the form of a bewitching pair of blue eyes looking into his across the manager's desk as she inquired about a safety deposit box. These soon became the adoring eyes of his betrothed.

So, life was good, as they say, to Harold John. Similar sentiments were running through his head one fine morning as he sat at his desk, blissfully unaware of the letter amongst the mail in front of him. It was written in terrible handwriting and short, to the point. Its author – the bank robber. *The murdering bank robber!* He wanted more money, which he knew Harold John could easily get his hands on, or else he'd be *'singin like a canary'*. At this point of reading, Harold John was confused, but the next words on the page sent an icy chill down his spine, *'bout you bein in on job wiv us'*.

The following days were a nightmare of indecision. Sleepless nights. Harold John even considered (for a brief moment) taking the money from the safe and leaving it at the place designated in the letter. Or should he go to the police? But what if they believed the robber's story, not his?

Oh, *what* to do, *where* to turn? And he was to be married in just a matter of weeks . . . But then everything was thankfully resolved, as the murdering robber was found and arrested.

When Harold John heard the news (no one in the bank talked of anything else) he could scarcely believe his luck, but he had only one day to savour the feeling before he was arrested for suspected bank robbery and accessory to murder.

The tide of public opinion quickly began to turn. It seemed too much of a coincidence that the week the robbery took place the safe contained more money than usual. Why had Harold John, usually such a quiet man, chased after a robber with such alacrity? To put him above suspicion? Someone mentioned Harold John's late-night walks. Another commented there'd been a good few break-ins lately. (He was his father's son, after all.)

No bewitching eyes came to gaze consolingly across the visiting table, but who could blame her for not wanting to consort with a suspected criminal? A mastermind of deception. How was she to know the truth?

Harold John Pinter's luck had run out.

Buster

'**S**ERIOUSLY, LIKE?' JOSH stared at his mum in disbelief.

'I've told him you'll do it. Needs a man to help him, so he does.'

Josh couldn't believe his ears. *Wee Joshie*, or *my wee boy*, what she called him to wind him up. Now she wanted him to muck out cows, he was *a man*.

It was the start of the summer hols, no way, like, he was spending them on his great uncle's farm.

'As you know, Liv,' (he had dropped 'Mum' since he'd turned sixteen, to wind *her* up) 'I've got a job.'

Buster wouldn't pay him, was hard up. At Christmas, Josh got a bag of sweets pressed into his hand. Nothing for Liv, who'd a turkey dinner for him, and a cake. Had to cart it all there on the bus. They took milk with them; Liv didn't trust Buster's, tutted about the cottage on the way home, 'Falling down round him, so it is.' A bucket in the porch Josh had to mind not to trip over; leaks everywhere, buckets and basins all over the place; ping, plopping when it rained, Buster's loud chomping on the cake.

'He's an old man, Joshie. We're all he has, so we are.'

Buster had been in hospital for an operation, 'gettin' the aul hip done', as he called it. Josh got him into the cottage on his crutches; he lowered himself, groaning, onto the ancient sofa. Liv said she'd put the kettle on. 'Aye, could dae wi' wettin' m'whistle.'

Josh helped Liv clean the cottage. 'Can't let carers see the state of this, so we can't,' she said. The bathroom was the worse, like, the toilet totally gross. The bath taps didn't turn. No shower. 'Where does he . . . ?' Josh realised. '*Ugh*, what a minger!' 'At the sink,' Liv replied. 'Pass us the bleach. Stop making a fuss, you're such a ginny, so you are.' Josh frowned. '*Huh?* What's a ginny?' Sounded like something Buster would say; Josh needed an app for his phone, translate Country into English.

'Ye know onything 'bout beasts, lad?'

Was it a trick question, like? Same way kids got asked, where'd eggs come from? 'Walking burgers,' Josh wanted to reply, for a laugh, like, but Buster might think he was giving him lip. 'Promise you'll behave, no messin,' Liv had said when he'd left the flat, running to catch the bus.

'Fill a bucket.' Buster pointed to a large container, then to a gate at the other side of the yard. The cows stood behind it were pushing into each other, roaring. *Huh?* Couldn't expect Josh to go in with them, what if there was a bull! 'They all cows, like?' Buster nodded, 'Aye, all coos. Pour it inta the basins.'

The cows crowded round him as he emptied nuts into

the plastic troughs. No, no, Josh didn't like this! They were butting each other with their massive heads; he couldn't get out, was surrounded! 'Shoo, shoo, go on, shoo! Shoo!' When he got back over to the gate his trainers were – *ugh*, he'd stood in– 'Wash the dung off 'em o'er there,' Buster indicated a hose going into a trough.

Next day, a Ford Fiesta parked in the yard.

A woman in a blue uniform, tunic and trousers, was sat on the saggy sofa, talking to Buster. 'It's very important, Duncan,' Josh thought he'd been christened Buster, had said to Liv, 'Weird name, like, to call a baby.' Liv laughed so much she had a stitch in her side. Josh had wanted to ask how he got the nickname, but didn't want to get laughed at again, must be obvious, like, some way he couldn't see.

'. . . to exercise your hip every day.' The woman noticed him, in the doorway.

Josh felt his face colour, had to come into the room.

'Hello! You must be "*the lad*".'

Josh returned her smile. 'That's me.'

'I'm Hazel, Duncan's carer.'

She would be calling each morning and night. Her job was to . . . Buster was goggling the front of her tunic, the top buttons looked about to pop off, like, from the pressure of containing her boobs; Josh felt his face burn up, she'd caught him staring at them, which was totally unfair, like, 'cause Buster was plucking at a thread in the sofa arm, as if he'd been looking at it all along.

'Duncan has been telling me you help him wash at the bathroom sink. It will be a couple of weeks before he can have a bath.'

Josh could land him in it. '*Buster, have a bath?*' Ha, would serve him right, for acting all innocent, like, and Josh getting caught out. Buster narrowed his eyes at him – don't say nothing 'bout the bath taps not working.

The red Fiesta in the yard each day when Josh got there.

Hazel knelt in front of Buster, her hands on his leg. 'Now the other way, Duncan. How does that feel?' Buster's voice thick, 'Aye . . . it, it needed that.' The words catching in his throat, 'Aye . . . it did.'

The plumber hadn't turned up. Buster on the phone, 'What's keepin' ye? Liv rang ye weeks back. What ye mean it's nae a 'mergency? Course it is, I cannae hae a bath!' Josh chuckled to himself; Buster didn't want Hazel finding out he was a minger.

'Where are ye, lad?'

'Ge' the soap an' a towel.'

Buster hobbled outside on his crutches, over to the water trough.

Took off his shirt and vest. 'Help me aff wi' m'troosers.' *Ugh.* Massive stained Y-fronts. 'Turn on the hose, lad.' He gotta be joking, the water'd be freezing, like! 'Turn it on!' roared Buster, dropped the pants to his ankles. *Ugh.* Josh kept his head turned away. Buster bellowed, 'Ye're washin' the yard nae me!' Josh had to look at him; he was covered in hair, like. *Ugh!*

Buster towelled himself down, hobbled back inside, told Josh to fetch clean clothes from his press.

Josh walked to the village for groceries. 'Ge's a receipt, lad.' Buster counted the change when he got back; paid Josh a tenner a day, beamed at him, as if he was being real generous, like. Josh knew he'd got it bad for Hazel when he said, 'Here, gae Liv this,' pressed a wad of notes into his hand. 'Tell her tae ge' me new threads.'

'Still life in the old dog,' Josh laughed, passing on the message and money.

'What you mean?'

'He *likes* Hazel.'

Liv frowned.

'Does *she* like *him*?'

'Aye . . . I mean, yes.' Josh clapped his hand over his mouth. 'He's got me doing it, it'll be *aye* every other word.'

'How d'you know she likes him?'

The sound of laughter when Josh went in the house. '*He's a case, your uncle.*'

'What's with the Spanish Inquisition, like?'

Liv went with Josh; got the bus to Buster's.

A red car parked in the yard.

They were on the sofa, the backs of their heads above it. Buster must have trimmed his hair, Liv could see the collar of the new shirt she'd got him, so she could. The woman stood up as Liv came into the room.

'I'm Hazel,' a smile creasing her round face (a big, busty woman of . . . 'bout sixty, Liv reckoned). 'Duncan's carer.'

'L-Liv,' Buster stammered, his face flushed, 'I-I werenae expectin' ye.'

'Ah, Josh's mum.' The woman put a hand on her ample hip. 'That's a lovely lad you've got.'

A thick gold band on Hazel's wedding finger. Liv smiled back. 'I'll put the kettle on, so I will.'

Buster scarcely said two words. 'You from the village then?' Liv asked Hazel. Buster's face was beetroot; like a schoolboy, so he was, Liv smiled to herself, staring down into his mug, not letting his eyes drift to Hazel, thought he could fool Liv.

Hazel began talking about Buster's hip, how he'd been doing his exercises religiously twice a day, not like most she came across, she added with a hearty laugh.

'Wish I could do more to help.' Liv glanced around the room, which looked cleaner, tidier. 'I work nights. Zonked out all day, so I am.'

Hazel asked where she worked?

Just saying the factory's name made Liv feel weary. Sixteen years she'd been there, so she had. Covered the rent, the bills, never enough for a holiday. Liv's mam had looked after wee Joshie. Liv had missed so much of his growing up; had two jobs then, a cleaner as well, dead on her feet. Been only way to pay 'his' debts, left her high and dry, so he had, six months preggers.

Buster's eyes followed Hazel as she went to refill the teapot. Dear love him, he'd got it bad, so he had. But he knew she was married, no missing that wedding ring.

'You making a farmer out of Joshie then?'

'If I tull him they was bullocks he wouldnae gae near them.'

'*He's a case, is Buster.*' What Liv's mam used to say. Had a soft spot for her brother, had done everything for him; said in the hospice, '*You'll look out for him, won't you, Liv.*'

Josh appeared in the doorway.

'Coos all fed, lad?'

Buster caught Liv's eye, chuckling.

He was wearing Buster's wellington boots, looked like he could fit both his legs into one of them, so he could, made him look ten again, bless him.

'*What?*' Josh's brow wrinkled up. 'What's funny, like?'

'We'll have to get you a tweed cap, so we will, now you're a farmer.'

The plumber came, no more 'showers' in the yard. Josh helped his great uncle onto the stool in the bath, poured jugs of water over him. Buster frowned when the bill came, 'But ye on'y put on a set o' taps.' The plumber looked annoyed, 'Them's the cheapest ye get.' Josh showed him out. He got into his van, muttering, 'Miserable aul . . . an' him loaded.' *Huh?* Josh must've misheard; couldn't mean Buster, in his 'old hut' as Liv called it, with his leaky roof and nine cows.

'Where are ye, lad?'

Buster leant heavier on his crutch, getting something out of his back pocket; pressed a twenty quid note into Josh's hand. Extra pay, happy days! Josh was about to say, Ta very much.

'Ge' us a bunch o' flowers.'

Josh chuckled to himself as he ate his tea.

'What?' said Liv.

He told her about the flowers.

'Lost his head, so he has.'

Josh put on Buster's deep voice. 'Aye, he's right fond o' Hazel. Aye, a fine woman, that she is.'

Liv laughed.

'Wants to get his hands on her bazookas.'

'Josh!'

'Well, he does, like.'

'Just as well she's married,' said Liv.

'That time Eric took me to Blackpool . . . I met my Eric at . . .' Josh knew Buster was dead jealous, like, his foot twitching, sat in his new clobber, on the sofa.

'Nah, she's not.'

'What you mean?' said Liv.

'. . . my Eric's grave.'

'She's a what-you-call-it? A widow, like.'

'Can't get down on one knee, I'll have to do it for him,' Josh laughed, 'same's I've to do everything, like.'

Liv had gone all weird, staring at him as if he'd grew two heads.

'What?'

'He can't marry her.'

You'd think she'd be happy, like, wouldn't have to cart Christmas dinner to him no more, no more him on the phone wanting her to do things for him, no more scrubbing his minging bathroom.

'She's a gold digger. *Must* be.'

Josh choked on his pasta.

'Yeah, right; he's mega rich, like. She's after "the hut" and three fields.' Josh knew farmers usually had lots of land, like the ones on that programme Liv watched, *Country- something*. Josh was glad Buster had just three fields, 'cause he had to walk round them with this ton weight knapsack thing on his back, zapping weeds.

'He *can't* marry her,' Liv said again.

She explained how Buster had sold land to a builder, years back. Got a blank cheque for it.

'Your inher'tance, Josh, so it is.'

Josh walked across the field to the hedge. Hadn't paid no attention to the houses before, been too busy zapping. The village came right to the back of Buster's fields, like Liv said. Josh had googled blank cheque: *An unlimited amount of money*.

The sound of an engine; that'd be Hazel.

She got out of her car.

Seen him in the field; waved.

Josh waved back, watched her go in the cracked door of the cottage. 'She don't know he's rich,' he'd told Liv. 'She's lonely, that's reason she likes him.' Liv had shook her head real slow, as if he'd not got a clue, but Hazel said Eric's name all the time, like, any chance she got. Josh could tell she was real lonely.

'You can't stop them getting married,' he had told Liv.

'We'll see, so we will.'

Liv hadn't wanted to tell Josh, 'bout the money. He was gonna be a mechanic, was starting tech at the end of the summer. Car mad; was gonna be a Formula 1 mechanic. 'What you mean?' Liv had said. 'You know, on the telly, like, the car racing.' Some head-the-ball teacher had told him to dream big. Liv was lucky he wasn't like most of the kids round here, the dossers hangin' 'bout the flats, was a miracle he wasn't on the dope, so it was. He'd had a summer job since he was twelve, down the car wash. She'd worried it might change him, if he knew 'bout the money, 'bout how rich they'd be one day. He was just a kid, too young to get his head round it.

This Hazel woman lived in the village; everyone knew 'bout Buster's land going for building. Josh was in his room. Liv didn't know how to use the printer, would have to get him to do it, so she would.

'Huh?'

'A letter,' she repeated. 'To warn Buster.'

Josh stared at her, as if she'd lost her marbles.

'Your nan always looked out for him; he didn't give her nothing when he got the money, not a penny; didn't give us nothing neither. Mind when you was wee I'd two jobs. This Hazel woman has only known him five minutes and she'll get everything, so she will.'

Dear Buster,

Hazel is gold digger. Dont trust her. We near married. I found out in nick of time she was after money.

A well wisher.

'Seriously, Liv. Not a good idea, like.'

'Type and print it, Josh.'

'You can't go round . . . Prob'ly 'gainst the law, like.'

'I'm doing him a favour, so I am.'

'You don't know she's after his dosh.'

She tousled his hair, dear love him, he'd a lot to learn. 'He's eighty-two, all he talks 'bout is his corns and the price of cattle, tell me why else is she cosying up to him?'

'She's lonely, like.'

Liv shook her head. 'All an act, Joshie. You want Buster to get his heart broke?'

'No, but–'

She pointed at the poster of the car on his wall. 'What colour you gonna get?'

Josh poured nuts into the basins, quick as he could; was never quick enough. '*Shoo, shoo,*' one day they'd knock him over! He headed back to the gate, wellies flapping round his legs, were two sizes too big, like, but better than getting his trainers wrecked. Washed them with the hose. Hazel's Fiesta parked beside the trough; wheel arches were rusty, dents in the driver's door. *She'll get Buster to buy her a new one, so she will*, Liv would say.

Josh went over to the cottage.

In his sock soles he padded across the kitchen; the door was open into the other room, the backs of their heads above the sofa. 'This aul place is done. Gonna build me a new hoose . . .' Josh couldn't believe his ears; Liv would have a fit if she could hear him! 'Aye, a big hoose, wi' all them mod cons wemen want,' his voice all quivery, like. Josh had to put his hand over his mouth not to laugh out loud. The sly old dog, he was desperate, like, to get her to marry him.

Buster's head turned, seen Josh at the doorway, took a redner; his eyes narrowed, 'Did ye make a start on them gates, lad?'

This was gonna take forever, like, scraping off the flaky paint.

Hazel came out of the cottage; waved to him, drove away.

Josh looked at his watch; postie should be here soon, would get the letter before Buster seen it. Liv was acting mental, like, you couldn't park a Porsche outside the flats, would be stole the first night, and his mates wouldn't speak to him no more.

The postie!

Three envelopes. 'Ta, very much.'

There it was!

'What ye doin'?'

Buster behind him.

'Nothin'.'

'Why'd ye put my letter in yer pocket.'

Buster grabbed his arm real tight; shook it. Woah! Josh's whole body shook, like.

'Gae it tae me.'

Josh had to hand it over. Washed paint flakes from his wellies. What if he guessed it was from Liv?

'*Ye* sent this.'

Buster waved the letter in his face. '*Ye're* the gold digger.'

Josh moved fast, so Buster couldn't grab his arm again, but Buster stuck out his crutch, caught his foot; Josh stumbled, fell . . . scrambled up real quick, like, Buster shouting, 'Were ye, weren't it?' Had hold of him, shaking him again, Josh's teeth rattling, tried to pull away, but Buster got him in a headlock.

Josh elbowed his new hip; Buster's hold loosened. He broke free, tried to run in the stupid boots . . .

Hoovering.

Liv was keeping busy, to take her mind off it. Had tried

to sleep, *needed* to sleep, would be dead on her feet at work tonight, so she would.

He could have got the letter by now.

She'd hesitated before putting it in the postbox. 'You're not really gonna send it, like,' Josh had said. He didn't understand. Liv was doing Buster a favour, looking out for him, so she was.

She turned off the hoover; sat on Josh's bed. The poster of a sports car on the wall opposite. Was Josh's inher'tance, she'd no choice, wasn't fair, wasn't right, so it wasn't, her wee boy not getting his inher'tance.

Got her phone out of her pocket; she'd ring Josh, find out what Buster . . . What if he didn't believe the letter? What was she gonna do then? The phone began to ring, made her jump, her nerves were gone, so they were.

Private number

Who would that be? Wasn't anything to do with the letter, *couldn't* be about the letter. She shouldn't've sent it, was breaking out in a sweat; don't be daft, course won't be 'bout the letter.

It stopped ringing.

Bleeped.

A voice message.

'*Hello, Olivia. This is Hazel.*' Liv's pulse quickened; she must know about the letter, Buster must've told her 'bout it, they knew Liv sent it!

'*Your contact number was listed as Duncan's next of kin.*'

Something had happened to Buster? Liv shouldn't feel relieved. She liked him . . . kind of. He was an old man, these things happened, so they did; heart attacks, strokes.

*'I hope you don't mind me phoning. This is a bit awkward . . .
Duncan has grown fond of me.'*

Hazel would go on about how lonely she'd been since her husband died, would say she hoped Liv would be happy for them!

'Marriage proposals are an occupational hazard in my line of work. To save Duncan from embarrassment, I've arranged for another carer to take my place. I just wanted to let you know this was my last day . . .'

Liv played it again, to make sure she hadn't misunderstood. The letter!

The postie might not have been yet. Josh could get it before Buster seen it.

No answer.

Her heart was going like the hammers! Calm down, even if he *had* read it, Buster wouldn't know who it was from – her phone rang, that'd be Josh calling back.

Not his name on the screen.

'Hello,' Liv said, as airily as she could muster. What if he cut them off, didn't give them a penny, he'd leave it all to a charity just to spite them, wouldn't put it past him, so she wouldn't.

She waited for him to speak, could hear his ragged breathing; would be in a temper if he thought she'd sent the letter, had always had one on him. When Josh asked about his nickname she'd almost said, 'cause he broke so many noses, fighting, was a tearaway in his youth, so he was.

'I . . . I didnae . . . wasnae me, Liv.'

His voice was trembling.

'I, I jus' wanted him tae admit he writ it.'

Liv could pull this off. 'What you talking 'bout, Buster?' She focused on the sleek lines of the poster car to calm herself, had to convince him they had nothing to do with the letter; Josh had to get his inher'tance, so he did.

'He trupped Liv, I didnae push him or onythin'.'

Viv frowned. 'What you talking 'bout, Buster?'

'They took him in the amb'lance.'

It took a moment to sink in. 'J-Josh? You– you mean Josh?'

'He . . . he hit his heed on, on the trough. He trupped.'

She opened her mouth, but no words came out.

'He . . . he werenae breathin' when they . . . when they put him in the amb'lance.'

The phone fell from Liv's hand.

She tried to move, to stand. Was unable to function in any way.

Just sat there, as the phone tumbled across the carpet towards the wall opposite.

With the poster on it.

Of the Porsche.

In Her Sleep

'THE TIME? OH, let me see . . . Almost five o'clock. Goes so slow, when you're waiting, don't it? I've no patience. Not like my hubby; he's the most patient man you'd ever meet, has to be in his job. Never fidgets. "Can you not sit at peace for one minute?" he says, when we're in the car, but all I'm doing is tapping my feet, or pointing to things through the window . . . Sorry, what did you say? The traffic? Oh yes, this road is always busy. You must be new to town? I'm Patricia, by the way. Patsy for short . . . Pleased to meet you, too.

'You'll see me a lot around town. We're hard to miss, my partner George and me, in these red coats. "Here comes double trouble!" the fruit and veg man joked when we passed his shop on our rounds this morning. I stopped for a short chat. It's important, having good relations with the town folk. A word here, a smile there. George is a man of few words though, just likes to get on with the job. I had to jog to catch him up.

'He's fit for his age, is George. As I says to Hubby the

other night, there's no job like a traffic warden for keeping you in shape. It's a long way, round the town, and you have to do it in an hour to catch out the "zoners". That's cars in parking zones over their time limit. Then there's the "liners", who are kept well in line (excuse the pun) by George, who takes it personally when he spots a vehicle on double yellows, waits for the driver to return to give him a sharp word or two, instead of just leaving the ticket.

'Anyway, what was I saying . . . ah yes, the walking. It's great for the legs, all the exercise. Not that I have anything to complain about in that department. My shapely pins have *always* got a lot of attention, and not just from Hubby, let me tell you. Only the other day I was putting a fine under a wiper, when along saunters the driver, a *very* attractive young man. He had the usual excuses – he didn't know it was Pay and Display; where did it tell you? How was he meant to know? He kept his eyes on me, pretending the large Pay Station signs weren't there. The same old story – he didn't want to pay. It's only 50p to park for an hour!

'Anyway, I pleasantly pointed out the signs, explaining it was a standard £40 fine for non-display. He smiled, as if I was joking, and I must admit he had a fantastic set of teeth. In fact, if he hadn't been so young and otherwise fit, I would've swore they weren't real. I smiled back, as you do, though with my lips closed. I haven't been as lucky in the teeth department as I've been with the legs, to which his eyes had dropped, admiring the view below my skirt hem.

'What a charmer! He was sure he'd seen me modelling in one of them swimwear catalogues. Could I convince him otherwise! Anyway, we had a nice long chat. As I said before, it's important to get on with folk in my job. Not that his charm got him out of the fine. I stuck to my guns, even though his offer of a drink at The Pig and Swan was rather tempting . . . Pardon? I couldn't hear you with that lorry going past . . . No, I didn't say *at the crack of dawn*. **At The Pig and Swan.** You'd not know it of course, being new to town. On Station Road, you can't miss it. They do a very good ploughman's at lunchtime.

'Talking of Station Road; we had a real to-do last week. Didn't the lights only go and stop working at the crossroads, and me and George had to stand in. *Well*, if you seen the trouble we had getting folk to follow *very* simple hand signals. I almost got sandwiched between a Mini and a Transit van. I would *really* love to pop a few Highway Code questions at these so-called "drivers", I remember thinking, but they didn't give me the chance, jumping out of their vehicles and getting stuck into each other like nobody's business.

'The girl in the Mini wanted to know what the van driver thought he was doing. Was he blind? Did he not see *she* was the one being signalled to turn left? To which the van driver replied, *she* was the one with the sight defect, or else plain thick, as it was *him* who was getting the go ahead to turn right. The Mini girl didn't like this reply, particularly the "thick" part, feeling a case of whiplash coming on from her emergency stop, but she wasn't to be outdone by the van driver, who was also rubbing his neck in an exaggerated manner and muttering about claims.

'At this point I stepped in, saying they would have to stop this nonsense and move their vehicles, which were blocking the road.

'"An' *what* in the name of Heaven," said the van driver, "were *you* doin'? Bleedin' dancin' about like Michael Jackson."

'To this I took offence, although perhaps I had got slightly carried away. You see, when I put on my white gloves and begin my hand manoeuvres, a little beat starts in my head, and before I know it my feet just seem to move of their own accord.

'Anyway, I ignored the van driver's rude comment, telling him if he wouldn't move his van, then I would do it for him, taking a step towards it; we had a bit of a tussle, with my hat getting knocked off in the process, and if it hadn't been for George retrieving it from the ground and escorting me to safety, I really *do not* know what would have happened. And funny enough, a similar incident involving a van – *oh*, would you listen to me, getting all het up. My heart's going nineteen to the dozen just thinking about it. Stress – that's what it is.

'It's everywhere these days, isn't it? Everyone's talking about stress, like someone just invented it. Have to take it in my stride, I keep telling myself. Part of the job, just like the uniform. In the evenings, Hubby says, "Have a relaxing bath, Patsy, a good long soak." What I'd rather do is fill a flask with tea and go for a nice drive in the country, make the most of the summer nights, but Hubby's usually too tired, and he's already spent all day on the road.

'Anyway, there's always someone doing something they shouldn't in the country, same as the town: blocking entries, no tax, double parked. Hubby shakes his head before I've even opened my mouth. I have to close my eyes and talk about something else. It's a bit like being in the police, I suppose, always being on the job.

'Actually, when you think of it, mine's a lot like a policewoman's job – smart uniform, plenty of walking, keeping drivers on the straight and narrow, so to speak. And the danger element, that's similar too. Folk can get abusive, I can tell you, when you give them a ticket. That's why we're in pairs. Although George is always wandering away on his own. Sometimes, he disappears for hours on end. His ear problem plays up on him; he has this thing wrong with his eardrums you see. Some days I can't say even one word to him because the noise hurts them so much.

'What if I need backup though, and he's away off on his own? Folk can get aggressive, I can tell you, about a little fine. You'd think it was *£300*, not £30, the way they react. They don't take it kindly, my pointing this out. I won't repeat what they say back.

'That's another thing you have to put up with in this job – bad language. Dearie me, I could write a cursing dictionary when I retire. Either that, or give lessons in lying. Yesterday, a cheeky young madam insisted she'd left her car within the allowed time in a one-hour zone, not sixty-six minutes as recorded in my notebook. "Jus' an hour. *I swear*," she said, "on me mother's grave." "Would that be the same mother," I replied, "who was sat at the table next mine at bingo last night?"

'But all in all, a traffic warden isn't a bad job. Though people look at you strange when you say you enjoy your work. Folk are hard to understand sometimes, aren't they? Like the day someone stuck a sheet of paper on the back of my coat as I treated myself to a lunchtime ploughman's. I don't know how they did it without me noticing; I'm usually so sharp.

'All afternoon I got funny looks and sniggers. "SADIST" it said, which I thought *very* peculiar. I've always counted myself the happy-go-lucky type. In fact, the last time I was *really* sad was, oh, must be over two years ago now when little Gilbert died. That was a *very* sad time. Pardon? . . . No, we don't have children. Gilbert is, *was*, our gerbil. Murdered. By next door's cat.

'So yes, on the whole, not a bad job. And I've Hubby to go home to. Not like George, who's had one or two close runs in his day (or so they say) but never made it up the aisle. I know I'm lucky, having Hubby to– Sorry, what did you say? My bus? No, it's a number 10 I'm waiting for.

'Have you your fare ready? They've no courtesy, bus drivers. Don't like being kept waiting for a minute. Like that time I couldn't find my purse in my bag. If you'd heard the sighs of the driver! I had to remind him it was people like me who paid his wages. I told him I wasn't happy about ticket prices going up. *80p* mine is now! Absolute daylight robbery!

'Say again . . . *Me?* No, I don't drive . . . Yes, I did try the test, but unfortunately it wasn't my day . . . Well, yes, I did try again, a couple of times. Well, five times, actually, it was a bit embarrassing right enough, with Hubby being a driving instructor – oh look, that's my bus. Nice meeting you! Take care now!'

Selford Gazette:

Traffic warden disappearance

Mrs Patricia (Patsy) Pooley, a well-known figure in our community, has been missing for 48 hours. The last sighting of Mrs Pooley (51) was around 5pm on Tuesday at Hill Road bus stop. The police are appealing for anyone who saw her that day (August 19th) to come forward. According to an eyewitness, a man appeared as she was about to board a bus, waving what seemed to be a parking fine, remonstrating with her, pointing towards the town centre, and she followed him in that direction. The man is described as white, around 40 years of age, with brown hair tied in a ponytail and dark clothing. The police are appealing for this person to come forward to assist with their enquiries.

Selford Gazette:

Arrest over traffic warden disappearance

Five days after the disappearance of Mrs Patricia Pooley (51) an arrest has been made. A previous suspect, who was the last person to be seen with Mrs Pooley, has been released from police custody. Her husband, Mr Reginald Pooley (53) was arrested today over the disappearance of his wife.

Selford Gazette:

Traffic warden murder trial

The trial of Mr Reginald Pooley concluded today at High Court. He was found guilty of murdering his wife of 28 years, Mrs Patricia Pooley, on August 19th 2022 by a unanimous jury verdict. The court heard how Mr Pooley (53) first became a police suspect when, contrary to his claim that he was at home on the evening of his wife's disappearance, his car was captured on CCTV travelling to a remote beauty spot. The victim's body was subsequently found hidden in the forest there.

According to Mrs Pooley's friends, the 51-year-old enjoyed evening drives with her husband, to 'de-stress' from the pressures of her job as local traffic warden; under this pretext it appears she was lured to her death.

The prosecution claimed it was a pre-meditated crime, referring to evidence from the accused's personal computer: *how to dispose of a body* had been googled. Mrs Pooley's colleague testified that in the week prior to her death she had said, and he quoted: 'Hubby only went and knocked the hair dryer into the tub when I was in it! Must want rid of me, ha, ha, what d'you think, Georgie?'

Mr Pooley will be sentenced next month.

He has shown no remorse for his wife's murder. His response on record:

'She even talked in her sleep.'

Bottle of Vodka

LATE AGAIN!

Just my luck, Bunty is on the ward when I arrive. She looks over, watching as I wash my hands. Pauline says swabs need to be done on two new admits, can I see to them? Bunty's eyes bore into me as I put on disposables. I pull the curtain around a bed, blocking her from view. No doubt I'll be called to see her later.

I rap the door.

Nurse Supervisor J. H. Bunting.

Bunty indicates to sit at the other side of the desk. Her mouth lifts at the corners in a sort of smile. Yes! I'm going to get the sympathy vote.

Since the accident, everyone in my ward knows about Mum. In a way it's a relief not having to pretend any more, not having to make up excuses why I can't socialise with the other nurses. Bunty has pulled me up a few times for my timekeeping with a quiet word, but I've been pushing it these past few weeks. Today, I was twenty minutes late.

'How is your mother, Sonya?' Bunty asks.

Still the same, I silently reply. Still drinking herself to death.

The day of the accident, I thought her liver had finally packed up. I rushed to her, lying on the kitchen floor, slipped in her vomit. At least the amount of alcohol in her blood would have dulled the pain when she fell. I could have done with something to ease mine. A dislocated hip hurts like hell, I can vouch for that. She got away with dehydration. We ended up in my ward at the hospital, in beds beside each other.

'She's okay, thanks,' I reply. What else do you say?

Sometimes I think, I'm twenty-five. You are twenty-five, Sonya! Not forty-five! You need a life of your own. Be like Dad, just leave. Walk out one day and don't go back. Maybe I flatter myself that she won't survive without me, getting her up and washed, making her eat, putting her to bed, stubbing out her ciggies properly.

'How's your hip?' Bunty asks.

I wish she would just get on with it, give me a telling off, or this time it could be a verbal warning, let me get back to the ward. A&E was chock-a-block last night, which means we get inundated with new patients. The old lady who was in the road incident will need her dressing changed. I hope someone's seen to it. She'll be looking out for me. I told her I'll see her before I clock off. She smiled, 'Your young man will be waiting for you at home.'

'The hip's fine now, one hundred percent,' I reply.

Bunty glances down at her desk. 'This is awkward, Sonya . . .'

I inwardly smile. Bunty isn't cut out to be a supervisor. She can't bring herself to tell me off about my timekeeping.

'We've had a complaint about you, from a colleague.'

I stare.

'It has been alleged that you were seen pocketing medication.'

I continue to stare, bewildered. 'I . . . I don't understand.'

'Are you still on painkillers, Sonya, prescribed painkillers for your hip?' she asks.

'No. Not for months. I've no pain in my hip now. It's completely healed.'

'What were you on?' she asks.

'Fentanyl.'

Bunty nods. 'Analgesics like fentanyl can be addictive, as you know. When people have problems in other areas of their lives they can begin to rely on drugs like these to help them cope.'

'But I would never.' My voice is unsteady. 'You're going to take their word for it, whoever . . . whoever made up these lies about me?'

'We have to investigate the allegation, Sonya. Patient welfare could be at risk.'

Her hands fiddle with a pen on the desk. 'I'm afraid I have to suspend you.'

She can't mean it! What will we do without my wage? I pay the rent!

Bunty reads my mind. 'You'll be on full pay while on suspension.'

I remember Bunty's soft heart. I can change her mind. 'At

least I won't have to tell Mum.' I try for the sympathy vote. 'She never remembers I'm a nurse.'

Bunty's face is concerned. 'You know, Sonya, there are people who can help.'

I force a smile. 'We've already done the Alcoholics Anonymous thing. She even went to a clinic for a while.'

Bunty shakes her head. 'I don't mean your mother. I mean for other addictions, for drug dependencies. What I'm saying is, if, and it is just an if, Sonya, *if* you need help, then it will be there for you.'

I had to give Bunty my pass; she told me not to go back to the ward. I walk past it on my way out.

Pauline is at the nurses' station beside the ward entrance; she looks up as I approach. 'Where'd you get to?'

I study her face. It isn't her who has it in for me.

Of course, it isn't her.

Jay!

It'll have been Jay who went to Bunty. Since I turned him down he's barely spoken to me. Thinks he's God's gift. I'll go back to Bunty, explain: 'I thought we could still be friends, seems he's had a thing about me for a while. It's been awkward, seeing each other in work every day. I can't believe he has done this though, that he would go to you, that he would make up these lies . . .'

'Ester is asking for you,' says Pauline.

When I don't move, she thinks I don't know who she means. 'Old lady. Road accident. Came in last night.'

I open my mouth, try to say it. *I'm not allowed.* They will all know soon, Pauline and the other nurses, that I've been suspended.

I walk down the ward towards Ester's bed. A smile breaks over her face when she sees me.

I have to keep myself together for the next few minutes. I'll ring Bunty when I get home, explain about Jay.

'Did you get your dressing changed?' I ask Ester.

She nods, adds in a stage whisper, 'She wasn't as gentle as you, my dear.'

She moves position on the bed, her eyes clouding.

'Is it very sore?'

She shakes her head. 'Not too bad.'

I check my watch. 'You'll get more painkillers in an hour. I'm going home now. One of the other nurses will bring you them.'

'Off home to your young man.'

The TV is on in the living room; I can hear it when I unlock the front door. Mum is sitting in the chair facing it, the back of her head showing. From behind she looks as if she is watching the programme.

I sit on the chair beside hers. Her cigarettes and lighter are on her lap as if she is about to light up. Her eyes are closed; mouth open. The noise of the TV doesn't bother her, just like I know if I were to reach over and shake her it won't make any difference either.

'I got suspended.'

The blare of the TV drowns out my words. I switch it off; reach down, untie my shoe.

'For this.' I show her the pill between my fingers.

She gives a small grunt.

'You want to know where I got it?'

She grunts again. Her eyelids flicker, but don't open, her head turning away.

'This lovely old lady came into the ward last night. She was knocked down by a motorbike. Her back was hurt, a nasty injury, especially at her age. She's on painkillers, you know like the ones I used to take for my hip. She got two of these pills this morning, it says so on her chart. I know, because I wrote it.'

I don't think about it when I'm doing it. My mind blanks out everything else. I give the patient one pill, chart two. I can usually hold it together until lunchtime, but by then my hands are trembling and I worry someone is going to notice. Lately, I can't make it that long, I'm already coming down by then. It's started making me careless, the panic I'm feeling that I'll not get any that day.

'I never used to understand you, Mum. But I do now. See this.' I show her the pill again. 'This is my bottle of vodka. This is what gets me through the day.'

Her eyes open. She has heard me!

Her gaze doesn't focus on me; she says something too slurred to make out, then she's asleep again.

I take my mobile from my pocket.

Bunty's secretary answers, puts me through.

It will just be Jay's word against mine.

Pauline and the others will tell Bunty about my mood swings when she asks them about me. It isn't Pauline who saw me taking the pills, but she'll give me away, saying I'm stressed one minute and hyper the next.

I can pull it off though.

His word against mine.

Ester will be looking at the ward clock, waiting for her next medication, being brave. 'Not too bad,' what Gran used to say about the pain, managing a smile, even at the end, when the cancer had gone right through her.

Bunty comes on the line.

'I . . .'

I know who has made up these lies about me and why.

I try to block out Ester's pain-filled eyes.

'Sonya?'

'I . . . need help.'

Digit

THE SMALL FUNCTION room of The Oak Hotel was upholstered in faded tapestry furnishing. Where they always had their work Christmas dinner. This year, Ryan had wanted to have it in the new wine bar, where he enjoyed long lunches (*networking,* as he called it), but Walter was in charge, and they always went to The Oak.

Walter's wife, Daphne, seemed to be enjoying herself, was usually nervous about making conversation with his colleagues and their other halves. Ryan had come alone, hadn't brought one of the glamorous girls Walter saw him driving round town with.

Ryan was seated at the head of the table. In Hector's chair. He bore a physical resemblance to his grandfather, but not in personality, as far as Walter could see in the ten months since he had joined the company. His arrival meant there were now fourteen in the firm, a far cry from the old days when it was just a handful of them; Walter and Hec fitting wooden shelving in grocers; slat wall for newsagents.

Ryan caught his eye. 'All right, Wally?'

All heads turned to Walter.

'You're very quiet,' Ryan continued. 'He's a slave driver at work.' This was directed at Daphne. 'What would we do without Wally to keep us right?'

Walter could sense Daphne's unease, pressed his knee against hers under the table. His work colleagues were used to it, Ryan's name for him, and derisory tone of voice.

Ryan clearly enjoyed pushing the boundary of respect – being the boss's grandson gave him that liberty, or so he thought. Didn't like being told what to do under Walter's management, testing his influence, using his family connection to offload work onto the others, taking long lunches with his current girlfriend. Everyone else respected Walter's quiet authority, but any comments about Ryan's poor timekeeping were met with indignation. Did Walter not want him to network?

It had been Walter's networking that had built the firm up to what it was. He had travelled beyond Belfast, distributing their card and new brochure, making contacts. They became retail designers – practical yet unusual shelving, display solutions, innovative lighting, even exterior signs and canopies. Walter had an eye for detail. Their reputation slowly grew. Their portfolio of jobs – the businesses they had transformed – were a source of pride to Walter.

Not like this place. The hotel function room had gloomy curtains and seating, everything worn, out-of-date. Walter's younger colleagues probably viewed him that way; had no idea what the company was like in the beginning. Plans drawn by hand, handwritten invoices, how Walter had struggled when they'd become computerised, had to go to night classes at the library; he did the bookkeeping, had to learn quickly.

Walter watched Ryan raise his glass to his lips. A slender wrist, fine-boned, same as Hec. At the start, when everyone had been hands-on, building display cabinets, fixing shelves to walls, Hec did all the intricate work. 'Should have been a surgeon,' Walter told him, dropping another screw, his hands like shovels in comparison to Hec's, who had laughed, 'Would pay better than this.'

Tough years. The time they did a new fit on the Shankill. The shop had been blown to smithereens just a week later. No insurance; they never got paid. The business almost went under. Two people had died in the blast, dozens injured. 'We're the lucky ones, Walter,' Hec had said.

Ryan clicked his fingers at a passing waiter. The firm would be handed to him on a plate. Hec had been delighted when his grandson joined the company after university, was thankful it would continue in the family name; his son, Ryan's father, had died in a boating accident. Ryan was his only heir.

Since his heart attack, the future of the company seemed to be forefront in Hec's mind, his voice anxious during their telephone conversations as he asked about Ryan. Walter could feel his own anxiety rising now at the thought of Hec almost not making it, of his getting to hospital just in time.

Walter couldn't tell Hec about Ryan's poor attitude and lack of commitment to the job in his grandfather's absence. He didn't need the stress as he recuperated. 'The old ticker's getting a re-fit,' Hec had joked about the stent. When he'd asked how Ryan was getting on, Walter had to say he was an asset to the company.

Ryan stood, ran a hand through his thick dark hair. Another physical likeness to his grandfather; even in his seventies Hec still had a full head, silvery white. And the way he walked, another similarity, tilted forward, same as Ryan, as he headed in the direction of the gents.

With Ryan absent from the table, Walter could feel himself relax, hadn't realised how tense he was. It surprised him how much Ryan could raise him, because he didn't have a temper, never had. He noticed when other men got angry, their flushed face, how they said things they'd no doubt regret afterwards, was glad he wasn't like that. If anything, Walter was too much the other way – soft, a pushover, 'mammy's boy,' his brothers had called him.

Did Ryan pick up on his softness, knew Walter wouldn't react? He shouldn't have let him off with deriding him in front of Daphne, should have said, *The name's Walter, Ryan, show some respect.* Walter knew it was the alcohol making him uptight and annoyed. He'd only had one pint, but wasn't a drinker; didn't want to feel like this, because he had to somehow get through these next few weeks or months, please God let it be just weeks, until Hec returned.

Ryan came back to the table, rapped his glass with a spoon. Walter fixed a smile on his face as Ryan gave the Christmas speech on Hec's behalf, thanking everyone for their hard work during the year, their dedication to the company. 'My grandfather has asked me to especially thank . . .' A stirring in Walter's chest, if he called him . . . Ryan met his eye. Walter stared back, *Go on, I dare you.* Ryan cleared his throat, 'To especially thank Walter, for running the company in his absence.'

Walter stood. 'A toast, to our wonderful boss. May he make a speedy recovery.' Raised his glass. 'To Hector.'

'A nice young man,' Daphne commented over a late break-fast. Ryan had sat beside her in the lounge after the meal, chatting, making her laugh. A glimpse of Hec in him, Walter told himself, who always made a point of speaking to everyone, putting them at their ease.

Walter was dreading Monday; it was the same each weekend, had never felt like this until Ryan came on the scene. He had to concentrate on these signs of Hec in him. Ryan was young, a work in progress, could grow more like Hec in personality, not just physical resemblance.

Ryan wasn't at his desk, a car game on his computer screen. Walter headed to the staff room to hang up his coat. The door was open.

'Such a *lovely* speech, Ryan.' Daphne's mimicked words were high-pitched. 'I'm sure your grandfather is proud of you. So *very* proud.'

'She either wants to shag me, or adopt me,' Ryan continued in his normal voice. 'What d'you think?'

Someone weakly laughed.

'Poor Wally. Imagine having to live with that squeaker.'

Walter went back to his desk, concentrated on his breathing, waiting for it to slow. *Let it go.* He had kept his cool up to now. Just another few weeks. Had felt his hands balling, had almost gone into the staff room, almost gone over to Ryan . . .

He somehow got through the day, and the next. At the end of the week, Ryan came over, lowered his head, his mouth next to Walter's ear. 'My office. Now.'

Hector had told Walter to use his office in his absence, but it hadn't felt right; when it had remained empty, Ryan had taken it upon himself to use it. On first seeing Ryan behind Hec's desk, Walter had barely been able to keep his cool. Was there this side to every man, a dormant temper waiting to be unleashed?

Walter stayed at his desk. *Breathe . . . breathe.*

Walked slowly to Hec's office.

Ryan tossed sheets of paper across the desk.

A bank statement.

Don't panic. Walter could feel his face colouring, giving him away.

Ryan leaned back in Hec's chair, put his hands behind his head. Gloating.

Walter opened his mouth to say, a supplier wanting cash payment, but Ryan would ask *which* supplier, would check it out.

Ryan smirked. Anger gathered in Walter's chest. Why was Ryan snooping in the accounts anyway?

'Not denying it then?'

He knew Walter was the only one authorised to sign cheques, to withdraw money.

'That's private mail, Ryan.'

'*Private?*' Ryan spat back. 'You mean *company* mail. *My* grandfather's company.'

'Hec knows about it.'

Ryan gave a humourless laugh. 'C'mon Wally, what d'you take me for?'

'Knew the ole boy was getting doddery, but *this?*' He indicated the bank statement. 'How long you worked here, Wally?'

Walter pictured himself going around the desk, his hand

closing around Ryan's throat, dragging him from the chair, forcing him against the wall, his mouth at Ryan's ear. *Leave it. You never saw this. Understood?*

'Thirty years, Wally? More?'

Breathe. Don't make this worse than it already is.

'How long has it been going on Wally? How long you been stealing from the company?' Ryan's voice shook with anger. 'Hec thinks the sun shines out of you.'

'Ryan—'

'Let's see what the police have to say about it,' reached for the phone.

Walter's hand got to it first, holding Ryan's gaze, a challenge. *I could warn him off, it might work, look at him, there's uncertainty in his eyes – didn't know ole Wally had it in him.* Almost said, *Leave it, Ryan,* but knew he wouldn't, knew he'd regain his composure, be on the phone to the police as soon as Walter left the room.

'Ring your grandfather first.' Walter handed him the phone. 'Will be less stressful for him, hearing it from you.'

Walter went back to his desk.

Breathe . . . breathe.

The accountant had questioned it at the start, the amount withdrawn each month. Walter had explained a supplier wanted cash payment, included a fake invoice each month in the books from then on.

Ryan would be eagerly telling Hec what he had discovered, gloating, as he revealed who the culprit was. Hec would wait until Ryan said his piece, wouldn't interrupt, because that was his way. Walter had never seen Hec lose his temper, in all the years he'd known him, and it wasn't as if he never had reason.

The others turned off their computers, got their coats, chatted about the weekend.

'See you Monday, Walter.'

The door closed behind them.

Ryan emerged from Hec's office, strode towards Walter.

Eyeballed him from the other side of the desk, his face blazing, clearly too angry to speak. Instead, put two fingers in a V-shape to his eyes, pointed them at Walter – *I'm watching you*.

The outside door slammed behind him.

Walter knew how the conversation with his grandfather would have played out. Once Ryan's rant was over, there'd have been a silence. Ryan would have been confused, why was Hec not shouting, telling Ryan to phone the police! In his usual soft tone, Hec would have told Ryan he'd sort it out when he got back. He trusted Walter. The accounts had always been his department; if he had made cash withdrawals there would be an explanation.

Walter was still in charge.

If Walter had dreaded Mondays before, now it seemed impossible that he'd be able to go in after the weekend. How were he and Ryan going to work together?

On Sunday morning, he got a phone call from Hec's wife.

Walter struggled to take in what she was saying.

Hector had died in his sleep.

At the funeral service, Ryan was outside the church with his mother and stepfather, shaking hands, receiving condolences. Ryan was civil to Daphne, Walter had to give him that. A stony silence, his response to Walter's expressed sympathy.

Ryan read the eulogy. Daphne passed Walter tissues, tears in free flow down his cheeks; let them pour, Walter didn't care who saw. Ryan couldn't hold it together either, part way through reading his voice quivered, then stopped, his eyes filling. His mother had to take his place.

As they stood at the graveside, Ryan was again overcome, wiped away tears with his fingers. His stepfather put his hand on his arm, a nerve visibly jumping in his neck, whispering in his ear. Walter lip-read – 'You're making a show of us. Pull yourself together!' Ryan's face flinched. Walter knew Hec hadn't liked Ryan's stepfather, had tried to persuade his daughter-in-law not to marry him.

This was Ryan's father figure.

His role model.

At work the next day, Ryan didn't give Walter time to take off his coat.

'My office.'

Ryan didn't look at him, clearly couldn't bring himself to, addressed the space between them.

'You helped build this company to what it is. For that reason, and because my grandfather held you in high regard, I'm giving you the opportunity to pay back the money.'

Walter took an envelope from his pocket, slid it across the desk.

Ryan's name on it in Hec's spidery, unmistakable handwriting.

Different emotions flitted across Ryan's face as he read the letter – curiosity, shock, disbelief.

'You just *hand it over*?'

Walter nodded.

'How long?'

'From the start . . . near enough.'

When he first came through the door, Walter had thought he was a potential customer.

A donation, for the prisoners' wives, he'd called it.

Ryan's eyes scanned the letter again.

Hec must have written it after Ryan phoned him about the bank statement, a note with it. *Just in case the old ticker doesn't like the re-fit.* Was on the mat when Walter got home from the funeral.

'The police?' said Ryan.

Walter shook his head.

Hec knew someone in the force. Had said he runs the streets, said they couldn't touch him. 'Near enough said we'd have to pay, Walter. Off the record, of course. If we make a complaint – *put it like this, he likes a good fire.*'

'But we can't afford to,' Walter had replied.

The office was torched after they missed the first payment. A petrol bomb through the window. Luckily, it petered out, just smoke damage.

A note.

TASTER

They began to pay.

Had heard stories, realised who they were dealing with.

'You just *hand it over*?' Ryan repeated, his brow scrunching in disbelief.

Walter knew this was the way it would go, that Ryan wouldn't want to continue, and he understood why not, it made Walter sick to his stomach, the amount they'd paid over the years. But they'd no choice.

'It's called *protection money* for a reason, Ryan.'

'I'm coming with you, Wally.'

'No.'

'I think you're forgetting who's boss here.'

Walter didn't forget, how could he, lying awake at night, dreading every single day at work. He'd been at the job centre, filled in application forms. Hadn't heard anything back. No interviews. Unsurprising, at his age.

'Get in the car, Wally.'

It'll be okay, Walter told himself as they drove. The same as usual, hand the envelope to the barman. No one took him under their notice, course they didn't, after all these years.

They turned into the pub car park. Even from outside you could tell it was a rough joint, a low, squat building with grilles over the small windows. Dim inside. Walter thought of the first time he'd walked through the door, went up to the bar as instructed, handed it over the counter.

Ryan parked the car; grabbed the envelope from Walter's lap. 'Ryan, what are you . . . ?' He was out of the car, striding towards the pub, '*Ryan!*'

He disappeared through the pub door. Walter followed, his heart picking up speed.

Every head turned in Ryan's direction, becoming silent, same as the first time Walter entered.

Ryan reached the bar counter, waved the package at the barman.

'Tell whoever collects this, it's over!'

The barman looked beyond him.

Ryan followed his gaze, hesitation in his eyes, as if noticing the men gathered at tables for the first time; their deadpan expressions.

Sweat trickled down Walter's back, his blood thudding in his ears.

'You hear!' Ryan waved the package at them.

Walter's heart – louder, faster – was this how Hec felt just before . . .

Ryan strode past Walter.

They got into the car.

Drove past the pub door.

Someone had come outside.

He looked the same, just balder. *A donation . . .*

'That him?' Ryan slowed the car. 'Look at him! Just a squirt!'

'Honest to God, Wally,' Ryan laughed. 'All the height of him.'

Ryan gave the man the finger, as he watched them drive away.

A week went by, then another.

Nothing happened.

Didn't stop Walter's sleepless nights, the office could be going up in flames at that very moment.

He knocked on Hec's office door, averting his eyes from Ryan's name now on it.

'*Another job?*' Ryan actually looked disappointed. 'But Wally, you've been here a . . .'

Walter nodded. Lifetime.

He couldn't wait to get out of Hec's office, to work out his notice, to never have to lay eyes on Ryan again.

'So, where,' Ryan began, but Walter had already turned to leave.

'Headhunted, that it, Wally?' Ryan called after him, laughing.

A full night's sleep.

Daphne smiling over breakfast, didn't say, but knew she saw the difference in him, the stress gone. She had been proud, could see it in her eyes, when he'd changed firm.

He glanced at his watch, better be off.

Parked in the city centre.

Got changed out of his suit in the car. Someone would recognise him one day on the pavement, a friend of Daphne's, a neighbour, one of his old clients.

Then again, he didn't recognise himself, if he caught a glimpse in a shop window.

Got washed in the public toilets at the end of the day. Changed back into his suit in the car. As long as the bills got paid. On the way home each day – Daphne wouldn't mind, would understand, would tell her tonight.

He took flowers to the graveyard. Someone was already there, crouched, placing a bouquet.

Walter went to turn, but Ryan had glanced over. He'd driven past Walter on the pavement in the city centre, a redhead in the passenger seat. A heart-fluttering moment. He hadn't recognised Walter in his uniform and cap.

They gazed at the headstone. *Loving grandfather.*

'I miss him.'

Ryan looked vulnerable as he spoke, same as he had at the funeral. That was the thing about Ryan, he caught you off guard, made you feel you were being too hard on him.

They stood with their own thoughts; memories.

'How's the new job? Slave driver, same as usual, eh Wally?'

'I got a note,' Ryan went on.

'*NICE CAR*'

When Ryan found out about the protection money, Walter had told him about the office being torched, how you didn't mess with these people.

'I've ordered another one,' Ryan laughed. 'Was thinking of changing anyway.'

'Ryan, you need to take it seriously!'

Ryan laughed again, clapped him on the shoulder. 'See you around, Wally.'

Walter took Daphne out for dinner; someone driving past as they left the wine bar, slowing, tooting the horn. 'Walter, is that . . . ?' Walter nodded. Yes, it was Ryan, in a new sports car. Pointing at it, giving Walter a thumbs up.

Back to sleepless nights.

He had to make Ryan realise who he was dealing with.

The office had been modernised, wafer-thin computers, too-bright lighting, white desks. Everyone pleased to see him.

Knocked on Hec's door. Ryan looked pleased to see him as well. 'What's with the sombre face, Wally?'

'Ryan–'

'I know why you're here, you're *worried* about me.' He put a hand on his heart. '*Shucks*, I'm touched.'

'Ryan, you don't understand, he'll not let it go. Your car was a warning.' Walter had to make him see, for Hector's sake. Ryan had his faults, but he had loved his grandfather. He wasn't a bad lad underneath, just had a lot to learn.

'The thing is, Ryan, Hec and I heard what he–'

'Wally, it's *my* business now.'

'But, Ryan–'

'Would you ever grow a pair, Wally!'

Temper rising in Walter, his hands clenching. *I could knock sense into him. . .* Couldn't believe he'd just thought that. *Breathe. Let it go. Breathe.*

He walked to the door, turned back, almost tried again, to tell him, to warn him, but knew he wouldn't listen.

'The name's Walter, Ryan. Show some respect.'

Months passed, and Walter tried to push it from his mind, because it was beginning to niggle; he and Hec had needlessly handed over the company's hard-earned money. Like him, Hec had been soft-natured, another 'mammy's boy'.

Torching Hec's car might have been the end of it, if they'd just rode it out. Walter got changed back into his suit, rolled up his uniform, started the car. Tried to push it from his mind, to think instead of Daphne, at the cooker, making dinner, looking forward to him coming home.

No aroma of cooking as he entered the house.

She was sitting at the kitchen table, turned her head towards him as he came through the door.

Pale.

Distress on her face.

She knew.

Someone must have seen him, recognised him!

Walter's breath caught in his throat; how would she ever forgive him, for the weeks, *months*, he'd lied to her. It was the pity he'd felt unable to bear, would be in her eyes each morning at breakfast, would be between them, unspeakable, always there.

'I bumped into . . . at the shop . . .'

Walter opened his mouth. Couldn't find the words.

'I . . . can't take it in.' Daphne looked vacantly at him.

'Daphne,' Walter began.

'The poor boy.'

Walter felt unsteady, sat down as she told him what had happened. *I've ordered another one*, Ryan had said about his car.

'Who would do such a thing, Walter?'

Ryan hadn't let Walter warn him, hadn't wanted to know the man he was dealing with wasn't into punishment beatings like his 'colleagues'.

Daphne slowly shook her head. 'It's so . . . barbaric.'

He and Hec knew they'd no choice but to pay when they'd heard his nickname.

'To cut off his . . .'

Ryan wouldn't listen, hadn't given Walter the chance to explain:

They call him Digit.

Beautiful

THE WOMAN SEARCHES her handbag; can't seem to find what she is looking for. Dorothy feels a flutter of hope. This stranger in her home, sitting on her settee, is mad. Lies – every word of what she has said, what she has claimed, is lies – the ranting of a madwoman.

She should never have let her in.

When the bell rang, Dorothy had expected it to be her friend, Helen. 'Ivan Hull live here?' asked the woman on the doorstep.

Dorothy had hesitated before nodding, trying not to wrinkle her nose at the unpleasant odour, taking in the wild look in the woman's eyes; pock-marked face; shoulder-length, unkempt hair; her torn coat.

The woman looked past Dorothy, as though expecting to see Ivan inside.

Dorothy's hand tightened its grip on the door. What could this woman possibly want with Ivan? 'He's not in. Can *I* help you?'

'An' who would you be?'

Dorothy was taken aback by the woman's rudeness.

'I'm his wife,' she replied.

The woman smiled; a horrible, forced smile. 'He's already got one a'them.'

It took a moment for Dorothy to realise what was happening. 'You've got the wrong house. It's a common name, Hull. You've got the wrong address.'

'Ivan!' The woman shouted past Dorothy. 'Get out here! I knows you're in there!'

She stepped back, looked up at the bedroom windows. '*Ivan!*'

Helen walked up the driveway.

Dorothy opened the door wider, let the woman in.

'What's going on?' Helen looked anxiously at Dorothy. 'Are you okay?'

'She's a friend of Ivan's.

Helen's brow furrowed, clearly thinking, *a friend?* She opened her mouth, but Dorothy got there first.

'I'll phone you later.'

The woman came down the stairs as Dorothy closed the door. 'Where is he?'

Dorothy followed her into the kitchen. 'I *told* you. He's not here.'

The woman pushed past her, going into the living room, looking behind the door.

'Stop it!' Dorothy burst out. 'He's not here!'

The woman went over to the fireplace, lifted the photo frame from it. Their wedding day in this awful woman's hands. Stared at it, as though soaking in every detail of their clothes, the flowers, their smiling faces. She began laughing, throwing back her head; tried to speak, but was laughing too hard. 'Tie – the tie,' she spluttered. 'Same bloody tie.'

The horrible smile again.

'He wore it when we was wed.'

The woman is still rummaging in her large handbag, can't find the 'evidence' she claims to have. Dorothy feels calmer now. Of course she can't find it, because it doesn't exist.

She becomes more frustrated, tipping the contents of the bag onto the settee, hunting through them, scattering scraps of paper, food wrappers, junk. She is clearly mentally ill. How on earth was Dorothy going to get rid of her? Should never have let her in. She would have shouted for a while, then gone away to annoy someone else.

She is frantic now, her hands in the empty bag, pulling the ripped lining inside out. What if she is dangerous? Dorothy should call the police.

'Ah, ha!' The woman extracts an envelope tangled in the lining. Something drops out of it, onto the carpet.

Dorothy picks up the photograph at her feet.

They are sitting on a bench in front of railings. A beach behind. Ivan is tanned, in shorts; the woman's face is sunburnt, her hair shorter. His arm is around her waist; neither of them is smiling, as though caught unexpectedly by whoever took the photograph.

'Week in Blackpool,' says the woman. 'None a'the wedding come out. Camera didn't work.' She turns her head towards the photograph on the mantelpiece. 'When?'

'When were it?' she repeats.

Dorothy's voice is a whisper. 'Last year.'

'It were me bought it. The tie.'

Dorothy had insisted he wear it. She had been ironing shirts for him, hanging them in his wardrobe. He was renting an apartment; his sales job involved a lot of travelling. A row of ties on a rail. Mostly navy or green, Dorothy had seen them before, except for one which stood out from the rest – lavender with pink squares.

'Perfect for the wedding.'

He had shaken his head. 'I'll get a new one.'

'Please, wear this one.' It was the exact same shade of pink as the flowers Dorothy had chosen for her bouquet.

He took her in his arms. 'Are you going to be this bossy when we're married?'

She had laughed, kissing him.

The woman unfolds a sheet of paper from the envelope, thrusts it in Dorothy's face.

Ivan used to write Dorothy love letters, when they first met. She had never even got a Valentine card before. 'A bit plain,' she had heard herself described by her aunt, but that was being kind. She had always known she was very plain, known from when she was a teenager and boys didn't even glance in her direction. She was bridesmaid at her friends' weddings. They said, 'You'll be next.'

As if she wasn't invisible.

She had met Ivan the week before her fortieth birthday. He had come into the office to ask about car insurance. He couldn't seem to take his eyes away from her; her fingers made mistakes on the computer keyboard, entering his details. It was too good to be true, she kept thinking, as he took her out to dinner; as they held hands in the park; as they planned their future together. She had reread some of his letters only last week.

My darling Dorothy

His handwriting was large and loopy. Very distinctive.

Ivan Hull

The signature on the marriage certificate in front of her.

'Me ma were sick.' The woman puts the certificate and photograph back into the envelope. 'I had to go an' look after her. When I gets back he'd scarpered. Took all his stuff, cleared the money out the bank.'

The woman carelessly throws her possessions back into her bag, except for the envelope, which she carefully places in last. This proof of her marriage is clearly important to her.

Dorothy realises the full implications.

Bigamy is a crime.

'Every bloody penny,' the woman continues. 'How were I meant to pay the rent, the bills? They took the telly, the cooker . . .'

Her gaze moves around the room, as though comparing her home with Dorothy's. The antiques – the ornaments and paintings left to Dorothy – fill the walls and furniture.

'This your house?'

'Yes.' Dorothy's voice is barely audible. 'It was my parents' house.'

The only regret Dorothy had on her wedding day was that her parents hadn't lived to see it, to see their daughter in her wedding dress. All brides are beautiful, she had heard said. 'It'll be the happiest day of your life,' her mother used to tell her when she was a little girl. What about afterwards, Dorothy had wondered.

He tells her every day that he loves her.

Every single day.

The woman is gazing at a painting on the wall.

The most valuable item in the room.

Dorothy clears her throat, regains her composure. 'He'll be home soon. I'll pack his things, so he's ready to go with you.'

She goes upstairs, gets a suitcase from the top of the wardrobe, fills it with Ivan's clothes.

Comes back down with the case.

'He shouldn't be long now.' Dorothy sits, smooths her skirt over her knees.

The woman fidgets with the strap of her handbag, twists it between her fingers.

'I'm sure Ivan feels terrible,' says Dorothy. 'About taking your money.'

'That will be the first thing he'll do.' Dorothy's lips move into a reassuring smile. 'Pay it back.'

A look of relief passes over the woman's face. Then a sneer of scepticism.

'In fact, I could write a cheque now,' Dorothy continues. 'That would be easier, wouldn't it? Then you wouldn't have to discuss it.'

She goes over to the sideboard.

Gets her cheque book.

Looks expectantly at her visitor.

The woman runs her tongue over her bottom lip. 'Two . . .' Her fingers worry harder at the bag strap. 'Two grand.'

Dorothy writes the cheque.

Hands it over.

'I'll make a cup of tea. He'll not be long. Then you can both be on your way.'

Dorothy puts cups and saucers on a tray; takes milk from the fridge.

As the kettle begins to boil, the sound of her leaving – footstep on the hall tiles, the click of the front door opening . . . closing.

The kettle noisily reaches boiling point.

Dorothy goes back into the other room.

There is still the smell in the air, of musty clothes and unwashed skin.

Dorothy rests her head against the chair back, closes her eyes.

The clock on the mantelpiece loudly ticks.

How many cheques will she be able to write? She mentally adds figures; savings, investments . . .

He loves her.

The clock chimes five o'clock.

He tells her every single day he loves her.

She sprays air freshener.

Takes the suitcase back upstairs.

Her husband will be home soon.

The Plague

I'VE GOT THE plague.

That's what it's like. Laughing at breakfast. Dead by noon. You'll have heard of famous people with it. Like Gary Frey. Or that pop star, what's-his-name, the girls swoon over. Do you know what he said? The lows are worth it for the highs. He must have been on a high when he said that, *obviously*.

Churchill – he's the other one you'll have heard about, him and his black dog. He just got downers though, no laughing at breakfast.

I would like a dog, but my mum's allergic. A collie. They're the cleverest dog you can get. That's what the pop guy meant, how good the highs are, when you aren't lying on your bedroom floor in the dark, when you're down the park with your dog, throwing sticks for him. 'Bring it back, good boy, Winston!'

Okay, so I have an imaginary dog. Maybe all depressed/ bipolar blokes have one. Mr Pop could have a Pekingese. They aren't as clever as collies though. 'Walk on your hind legs, Winston,' but he wasn't sure, making a face, as if to say it wasn't natural for a four-legged animal. 'They do it on *Britain's Got Talent*,' I tried to persuade him.

'*Please.*'

'Are you talking to me?' A woman passed me on the path.

'I'm training my dog.'

The woman looked around, shielding the sun from her eyes. 'Have you lost him?'

'He's a collie. Too clever to get lost.'

I was having one of my 'little conversations', as Mum calls them. You see, when I'm down, I don't speak, full stop. When I'm up, you can't shut me up.

If I hadn't stopped to talk to the woman, I wouldn't have been taking the shortcut home from the park at the exact same time an old geezer was getting his bag snatched.

He wasn't giving it up, not without a fight. Must have been stronger than he looked, was having a tug of war with the other guy, who was trying to pull it out of his hands. I shouted, 'Hey!' The thief stopped, stepped forward, lifted his hand, as if to offer it to me to shake; a blade flicked up from between his fingers, as if by magic.

I was going to be stabbed.

I-Was-Going-To-Be-Stabbed!

I hadn't seen a knife as sharp-looking as this since the night Mum locked away all the kitchen ones. You'd think I'd be pleased, wouldn't you? No more lying on my bedroom floor wondering if hanging would be painful, or if I took all my med in one go, would I just have a mega upper, or would it actually finish me off?

But I wasn't pleased; I was frightened. 'Give it to him!' I shouted at the old geezer.

You see, this was the sort of thing happened to me; I'd be minding my own business and trying not to feel too happy (if I felt only *a bit* happy, then maybe I'd feel only *a bit* depressed later) and things, *events*, like witnessing a robbery and almost being stabbed, just seemed to happen to me.

A cyclist appeared on the path, and the bag snatcher legged it.

The old geezer went over to a bench, breathing heavily, clutching tightly the enormous bag. What was he doing with a woman's handbag anyway? Gran had kept her savings and a carriage clock in hers. My great aunt had carted a stuffed hamster around in hers. Bet that's what this old geezer was doing, carrying his prized possessions round with him. All old folk were crazy.

He patted the bag on his knee, like you would a pet, pointed a finger. 'Not exactly the hero of the day, were you?'

Winston raised an ear.

'Give it to him.'

Just because *he* didn't mind being stabbed for a few quid and an old handbag. I remembered I was suicidal. Why wasn't I pleased someone else was going to finish me off? Should be a relief.

'Relief from what?' asked the old geezer. I must have said it out loud.

The doc told me not to be ashamed. 'I'm bipolar.'

The geezer frowned.

'You know, laughing at breakfast, dead by noon, like the . . .'

'It's *not* like the plague, Lee.' Mum tells me off for calling it that. 'The plague was an infection from *rats*, and you didn't take it at breakfast and die by lunchtime.'

But you did, they told us in History.

It was a week since the old geezer and the bag incident; I was in the park again with Winston, chasing birds. He was, that is – the feathered type. I was feeling happy (you know, normal, enjoying-taking-your-dog-for-a-walk-in-the-park-type happy), maybe the new med was starting to work. I wasn't skipping and punching the air with joy. I was just, you know, normal happy. Winston wasn't helping though, racing after a bird. When it flew up into a tree, he looked at me, puzzled, as if to say, what do I do now? I doubled over laughing.

'Woof! Woof!' Winston jumped into the air as another bird flew past. 'Woof! Woof!'

'What are you doing?'

A sultry voice behind me; who it belonged to would be hot, I just knew. She might have blonde hair. I liked blonde hair (I know, predictable!), pale skin and freckles.

'I'm just . . .'

Pink. She had bright pink hair. If she had freckles you couldn't see them because of her tan.

'Persecuting the birds,' she finished for me.

Persecuting? Some of her tan had got onto her white T-shirt.

She put her hands on her hips.

Her hair could be blonde, under the pink, and she could have been pale-skinned with freckles before she got sprayed.

'Why are you barking at them?'

I glanced at Winston. He looked up at me with an innocent expression. *Don't dare blame me.*

'I'm just feeling, you know, a bit. . . manic.'

She rolled her eyes. 'Not another one.'

'What do you mean?'

'My stepdad.' She sighed. 'Today, he painted my room yellow. Well, half of it, before he took a downer. That's what the whole house is – half painted, *every* room. I hate yellow.'

'You'd rather have pink.'

She looked at me as if I was totally thick. 'You think I'd want a *pink* bedroom?'

Winst tilted his head, confused.

She walked on.

'Are you stalking me?'

'What's he like? Your stepdad, when he's on a downer?'

'A *nightmare*. You always know what mood he's in, 'cause when he's up he never shuts up, like today when he was painting my room, he talked all the time. To himself. Out loud. When he's on a downer he's deathly quiet.'

Deathly quiet. 'Has he ever . . .'

'Tried to hang himself, but the rope broke. Sprained his ankle.'

It wasn't the pink girl's fault. It wasn't her talking about suicide that made me think about it, because I was still happy, running home, racing Winston.

Wasn't until the middle of the night, I started to slide. That's what it feels like, sliding down into a black hole you know there's no way out of, and you have to make it stop, you can't go into the hole, you know how bad it is down there, and you're getting out of bed, frantically searching in the wardrobe for where you hid it, and you know it doesn't hurt, not for the first few moments. Then all you have to do is wait.

There weren't many people about in the park today, no old geezers prepared to die for a few savings, or hot pink girls. I was feeling pretty normal, maybe my new med was starting to work. It was kind of boring though, even Winston looked fed up. I didn't want to go home; Mum was trying to put on a brave face. How did she know about the razor blade? Must search my room every day. She seemed to know I was going to use it last night, could tell by the way she looked at me this morning. *Don't do this to me, Lee.* Her eyes are always bleary, I give her sleepless nights.

Oh, *him* again. *Bag-man.* On the bench up ahead. Hugging his handbag on his knee like a child. Dead giveaway it had cash inside, might as well have a sign on his head, ROBBERS THIS WAY! I sped up, Winston at my heels, power walking past.

'Yo, ho!'

We pretended not to hear.

'I've something for you!'

Winston's ears pricked up.

He went to pat the bench for me to sit beside him. 'You don't still have it, do you? . . . You know, the . . .'

'I'm not contagious.'

He rummaged in the depths of the bag. I shuffled closer on the bench, tried to glimpse inside. Could be our lucky day, Winst!

He brought something out.

Handed me–!

A packet of Murray Mints.

Winst and I shared a look.

Another old codger appeared on the path.

'Hallo there!'

He stopped beside us, leaned heavily on his stick. 'This here your grandson you was tellin' us about?'

'Yes, this is Rupert.'

Winston raised an eyebrow.

'Hear you're gonna be a doctor, young man?'

Bag-man's elbow nudged my ribs.

I nodded.

The codger looked impressed. 'I've a rash, terrible itchy so it is.'

I looked at Bag-man to help me out.

'Actually, I'm gonna be an animal doctor. Granda forgets the word. Vet.'

I was having a 'little conversation' to beat all little conversations.

'Ah.' The codger looked less impressed.

'Animals can't tell you where it hurts.'

He was impressed again.

Pink appeared, coming towards us on the path. Her tan was fading. She had freckles on her nose! I was still hopeful about blonde hair.

'Hi!' The greeting escaped from my lips of its own accord.

She paused, looked awkward.

'Rupert's girlfriend.'

I wish. My face felt like an electric fire with all the bars on.

Pink walked on. My heart dropped into my shoes. Living with her stepdad meant she'd never look twice at me.

The codger raised his stick in farewell.

'Go after her,' said Bag-man.

'She's not interested in me, 'cause I've got the plague.'

He inched along the bench. 'But you said . . .'

'Not normal, I mean.'

'I'm never gonna be normal.' My voice caught in my throat.

Bag-man frowned. 'Why would you want to be normal?'

Out of bed, scrambling into clothes, down the stairs, quiet, quiet, don't wake Mum, bridge is waiting for me . . . river is waiting . . . How long will it take? Seconds? Minutes? How long do lungs take to fill? . . . Front door, locked, no key, back door, same, no! No! Have to get to . . . window, too small, can't squeeze through. '*Lee!*' Mum holding onto me, too strong, we sink to the floor, she rocks me, sobbing. 'It's okay, I'm here, it'll pass, Lee, I'm here, I'm here . . .'

'What if there was a fire, Winst?'

We were down the park again.

'All very well Mum being a jailer, but what if there was a fire, we wouldn't be able to get out. We'd burn to death Winst, you, me and Mum! Are you keeping a lookout for Pink?'

Oh no . . . up ahead. *Bag-man!* On his bench, the handbag beside him.

'C'mon, speed up Winst!'

Glanced back. He looked . . . asleep? Something not right, his head was slumped funny.

I touched his shoulder. Shook his shoulder . . . He wouldn't wake up. Ring for an ambulance, Lee!

They took him away. His bag was still on the bench. I looked up the hospital number on my phone. 'There's an old geezer being brought in. Please tell him Rupert has his bag.'

'Stop laughing, Winst. Okay, so I'm carrying a woman's handbag. No big deal. Stop it!'

Pink was sitting on the bench up ahead. I tucked the bag under my arm. Held it behind my back.

She burst out laughing.

'It's not mine. I'm minding it.'

'You're minding a handbag?'

Winston had a stitch.

'Why, is it full of cash?'

Might as well have a sign on my head: ROBBERS THIS WAY.

'*You're* not gonna rob me, are you?' Winston rolled his eyes. I know, shut up, Lee.

'Maybe,' she said, her hand going into her pocket, bringing something out. A blade flicked up, as if by magic, between her fingers. 'Don't look so shocked. I'm keeping it for. . .'

Her stepdad. What if I still had the plague when I was old?

'I'm going down the mall if you . . . There's a new milk-shake bar.'

She was asking me out! Winston couldn't believe it either, jumping in circles, doing somersaults.

'Meet you there. Something I need to do first.'

Winston sniffed the bag once she had gone. *Look in it. Bet it's got his wife's ashes inside.* 'No it doesn't, Winst.' *Prove it.* 'I'm not opening it.' He tilted his head to the side. *You know you want to.*

Clothes? *Women's* clothes?

'Bag-man must want to be Bag-woman. A cross-dresser. Or he might once have been a woman.' Winston looked confused. 'Or they could be his dead wife's! He loved her so much he carries her clothes around with him.' They looked new though – a skirt with sequins, a sparkly top. A pair of high heels. I tried to imagine Bag-man dressed in these. A wig at the bottom of the bag. A *blonde* wig. I pictured Pink's head turning, long flowing curls cascading over her shoulders, smiling at me.

The hospital.

No dogs allowed.

Winston pretended he didn't see the sign.

A long queue at the reception desk. 'Will we take a look around, Winst, maybe we'll see him?'

Along a corridor, then another. Two nurses watching someone being pushed towards them in a wheelchair. 'No one apparently, not a living relative.'

'Rupert!'

Bag-man's eyes lit up when he saw the bag. He beckoned with his hand, 'Come this way.'

The nurse helped him into bed.

He noticed me looking at the monitors. 'Just a little turn. Keeping me in one night for' – he jiggled his eyes – '*observation.* Thank goodness, I'll not miss . . . Talking of which,' he opened the bag, 'hope you haven't been . . .'

As if I'd want to dress up as a girl!

Brought out the wig, put it on his head. I glanced quickly around; no one seemed to be looking our way.

'What do you think?'

I nodded approval. Shared a look with Winst. Crazy. All old folk.

'Dead spit, aren't I?'

Completely bonkers.

'For Olivia.'

'Who?'

'Olivia Newton-John!'

'You should come to opening night on Friday.' He brought a flyer out of the bag. Golden Oldies Theatrical Company presents: *Grease the Musical*

He flicked the blonde tresses over his shoulders.

'Shame you didn't get to be John Travolta.'

He stared, as if *I* was the crazy one. 'Why would I want to be John Travolta?'

Dear Mum,

> By the time you get this I'll be gone. You've done everything you could, but this time it's for real. I know you swop my med at night. I know where you keep the real stuff. I'm a bit scared in case this doesn't work, in case it just gives me a mega upper. I love you. . .

'Why do you keep reading that?'

'Lee . . .'

'At least I'll not be low on vitamins.'

They'd made me sick all the next day. She'd double duped me. Probably slept with my med under her pillow.

'Don't think I'll ever face an orange again.'

'We need to talk, Lee. I know I promised we'd handle this together, but it's not working. Obviously, really not working!' She was getting hysterical. 'I'm going to tell the doctor you need to be admitted again. I can't cope with this! It's only a matter of time until . . .'

'But the new med's starting to work.'

'Lee.'

'I feel great today. Super. Fan-tas-tic!'

'Lee . . .'

I couldn't look at her – red eyes; she was so thin. Winston was at the door, waiting for me. 'Have to go, have to get down the park. I feel brill, one hundred percent. In fact, I was just thinking–'

'Don't say it!'

'What?'

'The lows are worth it for–'

'I wasn't going to say that.'

I bounded out the door, Winston under my feet, tripping me up.

'What were you going to say?' she called after me.

I turned.

Grinned.

'Who wants to be normal!'

Hobnobs

SOMEONE IS OPENING the door.

Her? **The one you watched move in?**

'Hi there. I done the windows for the last people, wondered if . . .'

'Yes.' Closes the door in my face.

That wasn't friendly. Mustn't like the look of you.

Think she lives alone.

Having a good snoop, are you Des? Getting an eyeful through the windows?

Books everywhere, piled high in the back bedroom. No toys around, someone with kids wouldn't have time for all them books.

Quite the detective, aren't you?

Don't seem to be a bloke around neither.

Let me guess, the bathroom will tell you that for certain. It'll have frosted window glass, you'll have to ask to use it.

Third time there, I ring the bell, ask would she mind?

See how well I know you.

She does mind, turns away, points to the stairs.

No shaving stuff in the cabinet; just women's clothes in the laundry bin.

She's at the bottom of the stairs, can't wait to get me out the door. Has nice hair – dark, long and shiny. Needs cut, hangs over her face.

Won't matter, pretty face or not. Not what you're here for.

'Settled in, then?'

You window cleaners are such a chatty lot.

'How much do I owe you?'

She keeps her head turned away. Knew she'd be the shy, nervous type, knew when I seen the books.

'Last lot paid in Hobnobs.'

Eye contact.

'Choccy ones.'

A twitch of her lips.

'Okay, *part* payment. That's the honest truth.'

A smile. I can only see half of it; have to stop my hand reaching out to push back her hair.

Stop pretending, Des, that it makes any difference what she looks like.

A tray next time on the step – tea and Digestives.

'Sorry to be a pain,' I say, when she answers the bell. 'D'you have any sugar?'

The door's left open behind her. She jumps when she turns round in the kitchen, almost drops the bowl.

'Sorry, didn't mean . . .'

The kitchen table is covered with sheets of paper; she's always here when I do the windows.

'Work from home, do you?'

She fumbles in a drawer for a spoon, her back to me.

'I . . . I'm a copy editor.'

You don't know what that means, do you Des? Tell me, what does it mean?

She brings out the tray next time.

'I do a bit of DIY, if you need anything done . . . any shelves put up?'

She knows I've seen the books everywhere; can't not see them through the windows.

Window cleaners – cheery, chatty peeping Toms, isn't that right, Des?

She comes upstairs to see the shelves. Looks like a library when she puts on the books. She smiles, turns her head quick, the hair curtain moves back.

What else do you see in the house, Des? Any jewellery? Antiques? Not much trade in books for you, is there?

She kneels, sorts a pile of books on the floor, her back to me. Knows I've seen. 'You're finished,' she says, wanting me to go.

I kneel beside her. She flinches when I touch her hair.

Petted her like a cat, did you Des? You always did like animals.

She pushes my hand away, grabs her hair, yanks it back so I'll get a good gawk at the birthmark on her cheek. Huge, size of your hand. Dark red; purple in parts. Like it were coloured in by a kid with crayons.

Not a pretty face then, but as I said, will hardly matter to you.

Tea and Hobnobs at the kitchen table.

I reach over, tuck her hair behind her ear.

I can guess what happens next, please spare me the sordid details.

She knows I'm at the bedroom window. I keep working, my blade moving across the glass. She unfastens another button of her blouse, continues slow. The skirt is quicker, falling when she unzips it, onto the floor. She walks across the room, knows how she looks in her underwear.

Cut the crap, Des, and tell me what's in the house. You've been through her things, haven't you? Course you have. Let me guess, a couple of credit cards. Any cash worth talking about?

'What age are you?' she asks, as we lie on her flowery duvet. I trace the curve of her hip with my finger.

'Twenty-four.'

Liar! Why do you do that, lie just for the sake of it?

'How long have you been a window cleaner?'

She's onto you, Des. Time to go.

'You miss bits,' she says.

'Twenty-eight.'

She laughs. 'What, you think I count the bits you miss?'

'*I'm* twenty-eight.'

She's still laughing, says she thought it was just women who lied about their age.

But you are a compulsive liar, Des. You can't tell the truth about anything, can you?

I say it quick before I change my mind. 'I were inside . . . in prison.'

She looks at me different, like I knew she would.

Just admit to the burglary, not the other, you know how you don't like to think about the other.

'Someone got hurt . . . I hurt someone. Didn't mean to. It were meant to be empty . . . the house.'

Her head lowers, hair falling forward; I can't see her face, can't see what she's thinking.

'I'm different now. I started doing this, started cleaning windows. Years . . . been straight for years. I'm different now.'

Don't be ridiculous, of course you're not different now. You know what's in her purse, don't you? You know if there's anything worthwhile in her jewellery box, because you can't help it, sure you can't, Des?

She puts her legs over the side of the bed, sits up.

'I'm different now.'

'You think I'm desperate. You think because of this,' she points at her face, hand shaking, 'you think I'll say okay, it doesn't matter; you think me that hard up!'

She grabs her T-shirt, struggles into it, pulls on her jeans.

I scramble over to the door.

'Let me past!'

I take hold of her hands. She *has* to listen to me. *Has* to let me explain. 'I were off my head on drugs. Didn't know what I were doing.'

'Let – me – go!'

Restraining women, Des, that's beneath even you.

She rushes down the stairs, opens the front door. She has no shoes on, but she'll not care as long as she gets away from me.

'I didn't have to tell you!' I shout after her down the stairs.

The front door slams closed behind her.

And you shouldn't have, Des. I don't know what got into you. Have a look in her jewellery box, you'll get a consolation prize there.

I love her.

No, you don't. Pull yourself together. Time to go.

I bury my face in her pillow, breathe in her scent, cover my ears.

You think you can block me out? Now you're really being ridiculous.

I get slowly up from the bed, put on my clothes.

Don't forget about the jewellery, Des. There must be *something* of value. Might as well take it with you. *Go on*, it'll make you feel better.

I open the front door, almost fall over her sitting on the step. Her head is on her knees, her arms clenched around them.

'I don't think you're desperate.'

Next you'll tell her you'll never lie again, that you'll be a good boy, good little Des.

'I love . . . I'm in love with you.'

Don't make me laugh! Heard that line in a soap opera, did you Des? Do you know how desperate *you* sound?

She lifts her head. 'You should have told me before. I can't . . .'

She can't trust me.

You don't want a freak like her anyway.

'Who is?' she says.

'I never spoke.'

'You said, "She's beautiful."'

Remember you're a stickler for the truth now, Des.

'I were talking about you to . . .' I point at my head. 'I hear my ma's voice.'

What, you're going to tell her about me? Oh, I see, trying for the sympathy vote, is that it? I know, tell her

**about your kitten, they liked that story, didn't they, the
prison shrinks, tell her how I filled the kitchen sink, how
I told you I'd been teaching your little pet to swim. Watch
Dessie dear, see how clever she is. Oh, she must have forgotten her technique . . .** *Oh no!* **. . . Ah well, never mind.**

'Have done, since I were taken into care.'

Better still, tell her about your *friend,* **in the home, the
one who liked little boys.**

'Ran away, when I were fourteen. Slept rough.'

Don't know why I'm telling her this, won't make no
difference.

'Know it don't excuse what . . .'

'I . . .' Her face says it for her.

She can't be with someone like me.

'If you'd told me . . . at the start.'

Nothing for you here, Des. Time to go.

'For what it's worth, I've never felt this way.'

**But you loved me, son. Still do, our bond can never
be broken.**

''Bout anyone.'

Her eyes are streaming, same as mine.

'Give me a chance, I'll prove . . .'

Her head lowers.

Time to go, son.

My feet drag along the garden path.

I put my hand on the gate latch.

'Des?' Her voice is a whisper.

Can't see her face, behind the hair curtain, can't see what
she's thinking. 'You . . .' Her voice wavers. 'You'll still . . . do
the windows?'

Don't read anything into that, she *just* wants clean–
'Long as there's Hobnobs going.'
Her lips twitch.
Oh, for–
Can't see them, but know they do.
Know she wants to smile.

The Spare Room

THE GIRL AT the till had black nails.

Edna thought at first she had a bruised nail, but they were all the same – painted black. The girl put the milk, loaf of bread and newspaper into a bag, her lips moving, but Edna was mesmerised by the nails, missing what she said.

A queue had formed behind Edna. She opened her purse, tried to guess how much she was being asked for. She brought out coins, handed them to the girl, who looked impatiently at her. Edna fumbled for more coins, dropping some.

The man behind her picked them up from the floor, helped her give the girl the right amount. Edna smiled her thanks. He was tall, even taller than Kenneth, touching her arm as she turned to walk away, pointing to her bag of shopping on the counter. Edna tapped her head – she'd forget it if it wasn't screwed on.

When she got home, she sat in her chair, waited for her aches and pains to subside, unfolded the newspaper.

The front-page headline: PENSIONER ROBBED AND

BEATEN *An eighty-one-year-old man was viciously attacked during a robbery at his home last night . . .* It gave the street name, just a few blocks away from Edna's. *This is the latest in a series of crimes against pensioners in the area . . .*

Kenneth had got her a new chain for her door. He had called in unexpectedly. Usually, she only saw him on Sunday afternoons with Susan and the children. He had put a leaflet into her hands. 'Promise you'll read it, Mum.' He had said something more, but his head was turning away. She followed him to the front door; he had fiddled with his new chain, sliding it on and off, pleased with it. Said he would see her on Sunday.

The leaflet about home security and safety was on her mantelpiece, with the bills, behind the jug.

Edna reread the newspaper story. The man who was robbed would recover. He was in hospital; if he was really bad it would say he was in intensive care.

She went into the kitchen, brought a box out of a cupboard. Twenty-pound notes inside, rolled in an elastic band – the electric money. Tucked the notes into her purse, put her coat back on.

The corner shop was even busier than before.

Edna bought a packet of tea bags. She already knew the price, counted the coins into the girl's hand. She turned to go, bumped into the person behind, the contents of her purse spilling onto the floor. Someone bent down to help her pick up the roll of notes and the coins. Edna put them slowly back into her purse, glanced along the people in the queue.

After, she went to the arcade. The shops here were often

mentioned in the paper, in reports of shoplifting. Some of the shop windows had posters in them: NO HOODIES. Kenneth would have a fit if he saw her here. Edna sat on a graffiti-covered bench in the centre of the arcade, opened her purse, unrolled her money, slowly counting the notes.

She walked home, not going to the park as she usually did in the afternoons, somehow resisting the temptation to glance back to see if she was being followed. Closed her front door behind her; gazed at Kenneth's new chain. The home security leaflet advised to always put your door chain on. To be cautious, even if the caller was wearing a uniform – police, DOE, water service.

She turned on the TV. A programme about decorating houses, which Edna sometimes watched when she wasn't at the park.

Weather permitting, she went at the same time each day, so that she reached the park and got herself seated on a bench just before the schools got out. A young mother often sat beside Edna. Her children played on the slide or the swings, running over to them every so often. A stranger passing would think, that's nice, a grandmother with her family, enjoying the afternoon sunshine.

The TV subtitles said red was the key colour this season. Edna shook her head at the garish walls on the screen, at the black curtains with red squares. You'd never get a good night's sleep in a room like that.

Kenneth's spare room was tastefully decorated. The curtains were pink and blue floral, a border to match around the walls. At Christmas, Edna had peeped in on the way back from the bathroom. The room was as nice as she remembered, a large window overlooking the garden. She had wanted to make sure it hadn't changed, turned into a store for the children's old toys. Thankfully, it was just the same, with the bed made up, brushes on the dressing-table.

Edna glanced around her sitting room. She wouldn't take much with her – just a few ornaments and pictures. Susan would be glad of her help with the children, once Edna had recovered, that was; she might be bedridden at the start.

Tomorrow was pension day; she would put the extra money in her purse and try again. She'd have to be patient, not expect something to happen immediately. Would only be her second day. The arcade was probably her best chance of success. Someone was knocked down on the pavement the other week coming out of it, their bag snatched.

Something was faintly ringing in the distance.

Edna strained to hear . . .

Her doorbell!

She stood, heart fluttering.

All she had to do was let them in.

Kenneth's face was annoyed; why wasn't her chain on?

Edna tapped her head, would forget it if . . . He had a key for her door, why was he ringing the bell anyway? Why was he not at work?

He followed her into the sitting room 'Promise me . . . extra careful . . . read the leaflet?' When she didn't respond, he put his hand on her arm, waited for her to look at him. 'You need to put the door chain on, Mum. *Never* let strangers in.'

'Kenneth, did you notice, next door's up for sale, she's going to live with her daughter.' He vaguely nodded, same way he always responded to her hints.

After he'd gone, Edna settled herself in her chair again, her gaze moving around the room. She would take the Aynsley vase with her, but not the jug at the other end of the mantlepiece, had never liked it, was chipped. The blue and pink flowers on the vase would match the spare room curtains.

At Kenneth's house at Christmas, the gravy and stuffing had been shop bought as usual; Edna had brought the cake and pudding, or it would no doubt have been the same. Edna had to say everything was delicious, had to smile and nod when Susan recommended a brand of frozen roast potatoes. They probably ate those quick – Edna searched for the right word – *ready* meals, each night. Edna would have their dinner ready for them coming home from work, would mind the children after school, wasn't right, them going to a stranger.

Edna glanced at the clock, thought of the newspaper headline: PENSIONER ROBBED AND . . . Maybe tonight she would get lucky. Tilted her head to listen, in case she was missing hearing the doorbell. Her gaze moved to the leaflet behind the jug: *Ensure all doors and windows are securely locked.* They mightn't ring the bell, instead look for another way in.

Next morning, she closed the kitchen window. The room was chilly, and leaving it open hadn't produced results. Sighed, as she made breakfast. But it was early days, she reminded herself; the arcade would be her best chance of success.

She was getting ready to leave the house. What was that? . . . There it was again, a sound coming from the direction of the hall.

Rap. Rap.

Someone was knocking on her door!

But it was only half past ten in the morning, robbers wouldn't . . . although, it said in the leaflet they could call at any time, pretend to be from the DOE, or the water board, not to be deceived by a uniform.

Edna's pulse quickened as she unlocked the front door, was about to open it. What if it was Kenneth, testing her again? He'd said he was off work this week.

She slid on the chain, opened the door a fraction.

Two men, dressed in suits.

Could pretend to be salesmen . . .

She slid off the chain, opened wide the door.

They followed her inside. She indicated for them to sit, collapsing into her chair, her blood pounding in her ears.

One of the men spoke, gesturing with his hand. Edna tried to concentrate on his lips, but her mind was racing as quickly as her heart; she wanted it over.

The other man got up, coming towards her; she gripped tighter to the chair arms, bracing herself.

He reached a sheet of paper to her, pointed at the large letters of the heading: THE KINGDOM OF GOD IS NIGH.

She went to the post office in the afternoon. Collected her pension, came straight home, couldn't face the arcade, was too tired, had had enough excitement for one day.

As the decorating programme ended, she noticed a car like Kenneth's through the sitting room window, stopping outside.

The faint ring of the doorbell.

She opened the door on the chain; was rewarded with a smile.

He followed her inside, his face animated, saying he had a surprise for her.

Edna beamed. This must be why he was off work. He was getting the spare room ready! Clearing out the wardrobe and cupboards, giving it a thorough clean, bless him.

'You're so good to me, son.'

He put his hand into his jacket pocket.

'You wear it all the time, even in bed. Anything happens, you feel unwell, or . . . just press your emergency button!'

He put a plastic fob on a cord over her head. 'I've set it up with my mobile number.'

The following day, it had begun to rain by the time Edna got to the arcade. No one was about the shops, although the slot machine place looked busy, activity in and out its door, the glass front steamed up. She could have a go on a fruit machine, her roll of notes on show in her purse, but her feet were damp, pains shooting up her legs.

The decorating programme was starting when she got back. Today it was the Laura Ashley look, floral curtains, similar to those in the spare room. Susan would be glad of her help around the house. It needed a good going over. At Christmas, Edna had run a finger along the bathroom shelf.

If only she had patio doors; Edna had heard robbers went about at night, trying them, because they were often unlocked.

She left the sitting room window ajar. Anyone walking along the pavement would see all they had to do was put their hand in, open it, climb through.

Lying in bed, unable to sleep; Edna almost went down to close and lock it. In the morning, she was exhausted, aching all over. She needed to go to the shop or the arcade, would never get a result sitting at her electric fire, but couldn't face the coldness outside. Hadn't the heart to watch her programme in the afternoon.

What was that?

The doorbell was faintly ringing. She lifted the emergency button from the mantelpiece, in case it was Kenneth.

He was cock-a-hoop she was wearing it, grinning, looking like the little boy he once was, back when he was kind to his mother. Barely through the door before he was leaving again, hadn't time for a cup of tea. 'I haven't spoken to anyone all day,' she felt like saying.

'Sorry I can't stay longer, Mum. I've to get to the paint shop before it closes. I'm changing the spare room into an office.'

Edna's thoughts were fuddled with shock – *an office*. She tore the button over her head, hurled it to the floor. Grabbed the home security leaflet on the mantelpiece, crumpled it into a ball, threw it on the floor as well. The small burst of satisfaction this gave her quickly dissolved, and she sank into her chair.

She must have dozed over after crying herself out, because a noise woke her. She glanced at the clock. It was evening, almost eight o'clock. There it was again . . .

Her doorbell.

It kept on ringing.

She slid on the chain.

A man on her doorstep.

The police.

His face was young, too young to be a policeman. His lips moved, but her eyes were on his uniform. *Be cautious, even if they are wearing a uniform. Ask for ID, then ring the number on it to confirm they are genuine.*

Edna closed the door on him. There would be more of them waiting on the pavement, waiting to rob and hurt her. It was too late for her plan.

Although . . . Kenneth hadn't changed the spare room yet.

She took off the chain, opened wide the door.

The man stepped into her hallway, followed by another one, also dressed as a policeman.

Edna backed away from them, into the sitting room, her legs almost giving way, holding onto the top of her chair. Her heart was trying to hammer its way out of her chest.

They came into the room after her; Edna gripped tighter to the chair, trying to stay upright. They were coming towards her . . . Their hands were on her. . . She was falling.

Her eyes opened. A face appeared in front of her – she gave a start – the fake policeman! Her hands moved up to shield her face. He took hold of them, lowered them, his lips moving, '. . . passed out . . . ambulance on its way . . . get you checked over.' His uniform was very realistic; her gaze moved over the crisp shirt and tie, the walkie-talkie attached to his pocket. Maybe he really was . . . 'You'll not tell Kenneth, sure you won't, my son, that I let you in!' The policeman's mouth downturned. 'I'm afraid that's why we're here, love. Sorry to have to tell you . . .'

The longest night of Edna's life.

They operated on him. Only one person at a time could sit with him in intensive care.

Critical hours.

Someone had tried to steal Kenneth's car outside the paint shop. He'd struggled with them, his coat caught in the car door, he'd been dragged, broken leg and ribs, a punctured lung. Tubes going into his chest. Edna hung on the doctor's every word, following his lips, '*air drainage . . . inflate the lung.*'

Edna didn't understand – did these not mean opposite things? He wasn't going to make it! Susan said he'd be fine, would just take time, but Edna knew she was only saying that to placate her.

After a month, Kenneth got out of hospital. Susan asked, would Edna mind coming to stay with them? She had to go back to work, was in the middle of a concentric merger, whatever that was, couldn't be off.

Edna gazed around the spare room. This was what she had wanted.

Kenneth would never be the same again. How could his poor lung ever be the same again? She had to fight back tears. The pink and blue roses on the spare room curtains rebuked her – this was *her* fault.

Kenneth had a brass bell beside his bed. It had a very loud peel, so Edna heard it each time he needed her, to bring him painkillers, to help him onto the commode. 'Just press your emergency button!' she joked about the bell, forced smile and cheeriness. His medication made him drowsy. He didn't seem able to take in anything she said to him, didn't seem to remember saying these words to her.

Edna cleaned and hoovered, made the children a snack after school. They obviously preferred going to wherever they went before; went into their bedrooms, closed the doors.

A van came with groceries each week. Tin foil containers that filled the freezer. Edna wrote a new list, fresh fruit and vegetables, made nutritional meals which would help get Kenneth back on his feet. She cleaned and hoovered and cooked. His leg was healing, had gone for an X-ray, but it was a different story with his lung, had shortness of breath, chest pain; Edna couldn't bear it.

He slowly began to improve. Edna got down on her knees to give thanks, her joints screaming in protest by the time she'd finished.

Her knees were worse anyway, with all the cleaning, only way to get a floor properly disinfected, the old-fashioned way, not the quick swish over Susan gave it once a week with a grubby mop.

Nail cuttings on the bathroom floor; so many slovenly habits. Edna knew they were Susan's because they were pink, the colour of her toenails. She should be sitting with her husband, cheering up Kenneth, helping Edna with the housework, but her daughter-in-law had started going out at night with her friends. Edna tried to show her how to make cottage pie, but she'd just laughed. No one commented now, no longer praised Edna's meals, took for granted they'd keep appearing on the table.

Kenneth was finally back on his feet again, could walk without crutches, although wouldn't be able to drive. He was returning to work, had got an automatic car.

He put his hand on Edna's. 'It's not safe, you living alone in your house, Mum. You're comfortable, aren't you, in the spare room? You can bring your TV.' A tear in his eye. 'We love having you here.'

Edna still watched the decorating programme in the afternoons.

Liked looking out for her favourite design – floral-printed curtains, pastel-painted walls. She wondered what colour scheme Kenneth had been planning for his office, would have been a shame to take down the lovely spare bedroom curtains. Her gaze moved along her mantelpiece, lingered on the Aynsley vase, admiring the pink and blue flowers.

From her kitchen came the waft of baking. She had made a cherry cake for Kenneth. His favourite.

Ah, there he was now, the sound of him letting himself in her front door.

He came to see her every day. Kept trying to change her mind, said it gave him sleepless nights, worrying about her, bless him. Said he would redecorate the spare room, was that the reason why she wouldn't come to live with them, that she didn't like the décor?

'Susan and the children will be expecting you home,' said Edna, as they finished their cups of tea, but still he sat on, tried again to talk her into moving in with them.

'You need the spare room for an office, son.'

'Mum, I've told you already, I'm not doing that now, it's *your* room. I've bought you a TV, it's got a great picture, a much bigger screen than . . .'

Lately, he looked thinner, had dark circles under his eyes.

'*Please* Mum, what do I have to say or do to change your mind?'

'I've my emergency button, Kenneth,' she put her hand on the cord around her neck, 'And I always put the door chain on, never let strangers in.'

'But, Mum–'

'Have another slice of cake, son.'

He was getting grey hairs at his temples, she noticed, as he wrung his hands together.

Must be from all the worrying.

Bless him.

Dear reader,

Thank you for choosing my book. I do so hope you enjoyed it. Reviews are very important to authors to promote their work. Please consider posting a review on sites such as Amazon and Goodreads. It would be greatly appreciated.

Acknowledgements

A huge thanks to my wonderful family and friends for their support and enthusiasm for my writing. Especially to my mother – first reader and biggest fan (not biased, of course!), my sister Joan, who looks forward to my new stories, and my long-suffering husband, Clive, who has to endure being constantly asked, 'How does this sound? What is another word for . . .?' Also, thanks to Trista Smith, for improving my manuscript with her copyediting skills.

Also by Rosemary Mairs:

A Recycled Marriage

'A gorgeous collection'

— The Book Commentary

From a mother meeting her son's killer, to a wife's despair and desire for revenge when her beloved cat dies, this is a collection of stories about troubled lives. The protagonists struggle to cope in adversity, some finding themselves capable of unexpected courage and resilience, but for others adapting to their difficult circumstances appears impossible.

'Like the short story master himself, Roald Dahl, you are led into a world where you sense that all is not right. The intents of the characters are revealed by degrees, the delivery of the twist shocking and unsettling'

— Rachel Deeming, Reader Views

About the author

Rosemary Mairs lives in County Antrim, Northern Ireland. She studied Psychology at Queen's University Belfast. Her stories have been published in anthologies and won prizes. *My Father's Hands* received The Society of Authors' ALCS Tom-Gallon Trust Award. Her debut collection *A Recycled Marriage* (Cinnamon Press, 2021), was an Eludia Award Finalist. It includes the semi-autobiographical *A Beginner's Guide to Stammering,* which was longlisted for the 2018 Bristol Prize. The Troubles feature in her work, highlighting the personal tragedies of sectarianism. *Basket of Eggs* reached the Michael McLaverty Short Story Award 2014 longlist. *Lily* won The Writers' Bureau Short Story Competition. Discover more about her books at www.rosemarymairs.com

Made in the USA
Las Vegas, NV
15 October 2024

96941281R00156